SILVER CREEK

WRITTEN BY: JACKIE BENNETT

ISBN: 9781962204170 (ebook) 9781962204163 (paperback)
9781962204224 (hardcover)

SILVER CREEK PACK SERIES
BOOK 1

This book is dedicated to Clover who worked diligently to make this book happen, Thank you!

To my own precious Aria and Kiera who are my world along with my precious Frederick.

To my family who inspired and helped me along the way.

To Hannah and all of those who are successful living life on their own terms.

Prologue

"CONFUZIE" Cassie yelled and began to run. Cassie ran hard, she had the spell ready to go just in case. She knew they had found her. She hadn't been practicing her craft and she hadn't shifted in over a year. She knew she wasn't strong enough to fight them. She knew now she had to protect the one thing in this world that was more important to her than anything. She had to protect Aria.

She was a flame burning through the dark woods. Her fiery red hair was twisting around her face as it fell out of its braid. She was in yellow sleep pants with a matching yellow pajama shirt and her feet were bare. She didn't feel the debris on the forest floor cutting into the bottoms of her feet. A branch tore her shirt cutting into her stomach, but she never felt it. "Confuzie," she yelled again.

Her emerald eyes filled with tears, Aria had just turned thirteen a few months ago and Cassie knew she, herself, would not make it through the night. She would not see her daughter again. She had to fight the despair threatening to cripple her. She had to believe it was alright if she never saw Aria again, so long as she knew her daughter was safe. She ran and repeated the spell "Confuzie" over and over again, pouring so much strength into it, her stride began to shorten. Another branch caught her sleep pants tearing them and her leg. She knew she could not protect her daughter and herself. She had already made her choice; her daughter would be safe. She only made it another 150 yards before they caught her.

Contents

Chapter 1

3 years later...

As they drove down the winding gravel road, Aria was in awe as she looked out the windshield at her surroundings. The trees were tall and green, and the underbrush was brown as October marched towards November. She thought the forest surrounding them looked wild and vast. It was beautiful, and unnerving. She felt as though the forest had eyes. She thought she was being silly, but she may not have thought it was silly if she could've seen the Caribbean blue eyes watching as her car passed by the expansive wilderness. She had been following the eighteen-wheeler for what seemed like a month. She knew the last 2,400 miles had actually only taken her and her father 4 days to travel, but it seemed never-ending. It would have taken him less time had he not had to wait for her. She had only had her license for a month and a cross-country journey was not the way she imagined honing her driving skills. Her father had insisted on open communication the entire trip, so she had a CB radio on the passenger seat. She was proud of herself; the trip had cemented her belief she had this driving thing down.

They came to a Y in the road that wasn't all that much bigger than the eighteen-wheeler she was following which carefully maneuvered to the right. She turned to follow, thinking that the forest had become darker somehow and figured it must be a trick of the light from the accumulating clouds and her imagination. They drove for a while longer when suddenly the road opened up into a large circular driveway with plenty of room for her dad to turn around and park the eighteen-wheeler. She stopped before the drive, giving him room to maneuver the large vehicle. Once she heard his air brakes engaged, she pulled up in front of the log and river rock house that looked like a ski resort chalet she had seen on TV. As she was getting out of her car a dark blue pickup truck pulled in behind them.

Her heart skipped a beat as her mom got out of the truck. She started to hyperventilate, her mom had been dead for years, there was no way this woman could be her mother. Her dad stopped dead in his tracks, his breath quickening, staring at her mom. The woman with her mother's face paused when she took in their utter shock.

"Cassie didn't tell you, did she?" the woman asked.

Aria's brain began to work again, this woman was the same height with the same medium build as her mother, Cassie, had been. She had long red hair pulled back into a ponytail, the same fiery shade as she remembered her mother's. The cheek bones, eyes, and mouth were all her mother, but the voice held a slight accent that her mom had not spoken with. "Tell, tell us?" Aria stammered.

"Well, no, Cassie never said that her sister was also her identical twin." Her dad sighed and ran his hand through his graying hair. "You just gave us a bit of a shock."

"I'm very sorry; I would've mentioned it during one of our conversations so you wouldn't have been so shocked, but I assumed you knew." The women began to walk towards them as she spoke. "I'm Katrina." She held out her hand to shake Aria's dad's hand. "It's nice to finally meet you face to face."

"I'm Joel." Aria's dad said, still staring at Katrina. "Nice to meet you too."

After greeting Joel, Katrina walked towards Aria. "Look at you." Katrina was surprised how much the young women in front of her resembled her and Cassie. Her own daughter had the same features except Kiera's eyes were grey and Arias were hazel. Both Cassie and Katrina had emerald green eyes. The only other difference was Aria's hair was a strawberry blonde where Katrina's daughter shared the same fiery red that she and Cassie had. Katrina held her arms open asking with the gesture if she could hug Aria. Aria embraced the aunt she had never known.

After they pulled apart, Katrina stared at Aria a bit longer before turning back to Joel. "Let me show you your new home." She started up the river rock walkway towards the front of the house. As she unlocked the door Aria felt exhilarated. Katrina flipped on the lights to a large yet cozy great room with a massive double-sided river rock fireplace in the middle reaching up to cathedral ceilings. The other side of the room was encased with glass. The view outside was breathtaking. The brown meadow gave way to what Aria imagined was a drop off with slate gray mountains tipped with snow piercing up towards the sky beyond the forest. On the main entrance side of the double-sided fireplace was a small mudroom with a closet to the right. On the left of the entrance was a large kitchen table with a bench and several chairs around it. Past that a little more towards the back was a kitchen that opened to the back of the huge fireplace where she thought a large sectional couch should go. The floors were slate stone tile in the main entrance, kitchen and mudroom, while everything else had soft red wood floors. Everything was in earthy tones making the large room seem cozy despite the open floor plan and the expansive gorgeous view of the mountains beyond.

"Wow." Joel said, stopping, so suddenly Aria ran into him.

"Dad!" She complained but stopped what she was about to say when she took in the same view as him.

"We should have come earlier Aria." Joel said, a sad note to his voice.

"Everything happens in due time." Katrina said.

Aria supposed that Katrina was saying they weren't meant to come earlier. She was right, Aria wouldn't have wanted to leave her grandmother, and her grandmother would never have left Philadelphia. That city was in Grandma Ann's bones. Aria smiled at the thought of Grandma in the middle of nowhere Montana. "I don't think Grandma Ann would have liked it here!"

Joel smiled back at his daughter, "you're right" he sighed, "mom would have hated not being close to town, unable to run to the market whenever she wanted." Joel was about to start walking towards the door on the far-left side of the great room when a thought occurred to him. "Katrina, with me on the road so much Aria will be alone up here. Will she be alright?" he looked at his daughter and continued, "What if the power goes out? She can't haul wood in a snowstorm."

"Relax, Joel." Katrina eyed her niece. Aria looked strong and capable in her blue jeans and green shirt with the brown unzipped hoodie keeping her warm from the autumn chill. "I think she could handle hauling some firewood, but she won't have to if it's too bad. The house has a generator, we live close by, and that holder next to the fireplace will hold enough wood to last her a long while. Each of the bedrooms had a small wood stove and a similar storage holder for wood. Besides that, nothing will come down that we won't be able to get through to get over to her. You two are family, and we always take care of our family around here."

Joel was about to ask another question when they heard doors slamming from outside. "That'll be the cavalry," Katrina grinned. "Let's get you unpacked." After quickly taking them through the rest of the house, they went outside to see 11 strong young men ranging from teenager to adult. This is Gage, Xavier, Kyle, Drew, Blake, Al, Randy, Steven, Brian, Chris, and Zac. They are neighbors and friends. We live in the house down the other section of the road. We have a smaller cabin near the house that Xavier and Gage live in. Brian and Chris are my sons, and your cousins." Katrina said, pointing at two young men with light red hair. Aria was in awe of the attractive young men standing before her. Her cousins and the others smiled at her and they shook Joel's hand as they passed him going toward the truck to start hauling in boxes. Aria felt her stomach tighten and give way to butterflies as the tall blonde, in dark jeans and a t-shirt, Katrina had introduced as Xavier, walked past her.

"She looks a lot like you and Kiera" Chris commented to the group at large while eyeing his mother.

"That she does. We'll have dinner and get to know each other in a bit. Let's get them unpacked for now." Katrina said, and laid out the unloading plan, walking with them towards the semi-trailer.

Hours later Aria and her father had everything moved into the large house. However, with the size of the rooms it still looked empty. Boxes were placed in the correct locations but there were several rooms that they didn't have plans for yet. Their small couch was dwarfed in the large open great room. Aria would have to tell her father they needed a large sectional.

Aria kept noticing Xavier, he had piercing blue eyes that looked like the clear blue Caribbean Sea she had seen once when her dad had taken her and her mom on vacation to Cozumel, Mexico. He had darker blonde hair and an amazing body as well and showed how strong he was by lifting heavy boxes with no strain. Aria hoped he had not noticed her looking at him. Breaking out of her distracting daydream about Xavier snuggled up with her on the large sectional they did not have yet, she headed up to take one last look at her box-strewn bedroom.

She walked into her bedroom with the spacious bath to one side and the walk-in closet to the other and she felt like she and her father had won the lottery. The bedroom had a glass wall facing the mountains just like the living room. The design of the house meant all four bedrooms had the same amazing view as the great room. She went over to a box labeled bedding and pulled out her sheets and quilt. She put her purple sheets on her bed and laid out the large patchwork quilt Grandma Ann had made her on top. She started to think about Xavier again as she laid her pillow at the top of the bed when a voice startled her.

"Kiera is here with the pizzas." A masculine voice said from behind her, making her jump. "I didn't mean to startle you."

Aria knew before she turned that the masculine voice belonged to Xavier. She tried not to blush and give away that he had interrupted her daydreaming about him.

"I wasn't expecting anyone to come up." Aria explained. "Who is Kiera?" She remembered one of the guys saying she looked like Kiera.

"Kiera is your cousin, she's Brian and Chris's little sister. She's 15 but she drives between the houses since this is all private property." Xavier explained, trying not to be obvious about checking her out. "Chris and Brian are 16, the same age as you and Gage.

"That's nice." Xavier pointed at the quilt she had just put on her bed.

"Thanks, my grandma made it for me out of some of my mom's things." Aria looked down at the quilt. "It makes me feel like I have a piece of her with me."

"Were you close to your mom?" Xavier asked.

"She was my best friend." Aria smiled, running her hand over the quilt remembering all of the good times she had enjoyed with her mother. "I loved her more than anything." Aria looked up at him, "Are you close with your mom?"

"My mom died when I was 2 months old." Xavier told her.

"Oh, I'm so sorry." Aria felt stupid, and wished she hadn't asked him. "Is that why you live at Katrina's with that other boy?"

"Yes and no. I lived with my grandparents until I was 14 but they were killed in a car accident with Gage's mom." Xavier explained, "It was after they died that we both moved in with your Aunt Katrina and Uncle Gabriel."

"Oh, I'm sorry." Aria grimaced inside, could she not think of something more profound to say then, I'm sorry.

"Don't be sorry, you had no way to know. Shall we?" he questioned, sweeping his hand in front of him to indicate she should go first.

"Sure, thanks." Aria said, moving past him out into the hallway. She tried not to blush as her arm brushed against him.

As Xavier watched her walk past him, his belly tightened. She was the most gorgeous female he had ever seen. She was average height, but her jeans clung to her, showing off a strong, well-proportioned body. Her long golden red braid fell down her back. He had caught her hazel eyes looking at him as they unloaded the truck, and he wondered if she was interested in him as well. That thought brought him up short, as he realized she didn't know. She had no idea what he was. Although, he thought, she should be one too. He stopped at the top of the stairs when this thought hit him. She was sixteen. Why hadn't she shifted when she hit puberty? Surely, she had been through puberty if the way she filled out her jeans was any indication.

Xavier slipped into the room behind Aria. He saw Kiera who was opening a box that filled the room with the mouthwatering smell of pizza. "What did you bring everyone else to eat shorty?" He said to her as he made his way over to swipe a piece.

"Very funny Xavier, I don't think you could even eat all of these pizzas." Kiera rolled her gray eyes at him as he grabbed a second piece of pizza. Gage pulled Kiera's attention when he came up on the other side of her and began opening the rest of the boxes. Xavier looked at Katrina as Kiera turned towards Gage to chastise him about opening all of the boxes at once. He nodded towards the front door and they both slipped out of the house.

Aria had noticed Xavier beam at the pretty red head who brought the pizza. Her cousin, Aria realized. She was beautiful, tall and lean, with vibrant red hair and intense gray eyes. Aria thought looking into her eyes was like looking into the eyes of a wolf she had seen at a nature reserve her parents had brought her to when she was in 6th grade. They held the depths of a vast untouched wilderness in them. She was distracted when her dad asked her what she thought of the house, the day, and if she thought she would be happy here. Joel launched into a list of concerns he had about leaving Aria in the middle of nowhere by herself for weeks at a time. She turned her full attention to her father and didn't see Xavier and Katrina slip out the door.

"How is it possible she hasn't changed yet?" Xavier asked Katrina once they were safely outside.

"I don't know but I have some thoughts." Katrina responded. "But I want to wait and speak to Gabriel when he returns before discussing them" she stopped looking hesitant.

"Just tell me Trina." Xavier growled. His anger rising unexpectedly.

"Don't take that tone with me young man," Katrina growled back. "You are not the alpha yet."

"I know, but please." He tried to look chastised knowing that Katrina would stop talking if he made her too mad.

"I think it has something to do with the witch gift." Katrina gave in.

Xavier's eyebrows rose. "You think Cassie put a spell on her to prevent her from changing?" Xavier was shocked.

"Yes, I think that some sort of spell was definitely used," Katrina glanced towards the house. "I can tell that she and her father have no idea what we are."

Xavier looked at Katrina, "Did Cassie have the witch gift, I thought that was just an exaggeration." He stopped and stared hard at her. "Do you have the witch gift?"

Katrina paused, "We'll talk more when Gabriel gets back later tonight." Katrina knew she needed to talk things over with Gabriel before she said anything to anyone. There was more at stake than just herself if the witch gift was exposed.

He nodded reluctantly and they walked back into the house in silent agreement.

As they headed back towards the house, Xavier was thinking about Gabriel's decision to go with tradition and train him to be the next alpha. Usually, it would have been one of Gabriel's own son's once Xavier's bloodline had died out leaving only a 14-year-old child behind. But Gabriel had seen something special, something extra, in Xavier and everyone on the council had agreed he was meant to be the next alpha. Gabriel's own sons would be valued members of the pack and council.

"Dad, you heard Katrina, I'll be fine." Aria was consoling Joel. Joel made his living as an over-the-road truck driver and would be leaving his young daughter alone for weeks at a time in the huge house surrounded by the forest and the mountains. It had never bothered him in the past. Before Cassie died, he dreaded leaving because he missed them but the two would often accompany him when Aria had school breaks. After Cassie died, they moved from upstate New York to live with his mother Ann in Philadelphia. Ann and Aria got along so well that he never worried about leaving his daughter. He would come home, and they would be full of tales about all the fun they'd had. Six months ago, Ann had started feeling tired, within four months the cancer had taken her. The day after the funeral Joel received his first letter from Katrina since Cassie's death. After two months of emails, phone calls, and deliberations, Joel and his daughter decided to move to Montana and get to know Cassie's family. The house and surrounding property technically belonged to Aria. Cheri and Richard, Cassie and Katrina's parents, had left it to Cassie or her descendants when they died in a car accident about 3 years earlier along with Xavier's grandparents Fred and Emma as well as Natasha, Gage's mom who had also been in the car.

"I know." Joel breathed in heavily, "but…"

"Dad," Aria cut him off. "I'm 16, I'll be fine. I only liked Philadelphia because Grandma lived there. I didn't have many friends at school and thanks to snap chat and Instagram I can keep in touch with the ones I did have." Joel sighed as the stubborn look of determination came into his daughter's hazel eyes. Aria was not one for large fits or dramatic scenes, she was just determined. Once she set her sights on something she had a quiet but fierce determination to follow through that was next to impossible to dissuade her from.

Aria looked around; she knew that her father loved his job and that he wanted to keep working to support them. There was some life insurance money but taking off work to care for Grandma Ann, two burials in 3 years, and moving 2,400 miles had surely cut into that.

Aria didn't know that her grandparents had left her money as well. Joel was going to do everything in his power to keep that money saved for Aria so when she wanted to go to college and start out on her own, she would have a nice little nest egg. He was going to meet with a trucking company in Missoula in three days and get signed on as an independent contractor. He would keep working and ensure his daughter was taken care of. Despite his reservations, he was certain that Katrina and the others would keep watch over Aria. Besides, Aria herself was 16 going on 45. He felt the tension begin to leave his shoulders as Katrina came through the door and started towards them. They had made him feel instantly at ease.

"I bet you are exhausted." Katrina smiled and put her hand on Joel's shoulder. "We'll help you clean up this mess and leave you be."

"No, we are grateful for all of the help, stay as long as you like." Joel's invitation was genuine.

She turned to Aria, "It's Thursday night. Your dad is going to go into Missoula on Monday, to sign up with Northwest Trucking. I can come by and bring you over to the high school, we can introduce you and turn in the paperwork your dad filled out."

Aria smiled at her aunt. "That sounds like a plan!"

The evening passed with the others telling Aria and Joel about the nearby town of Silver Creek and the small high school where kids from the town and neighboring communities attended. The others had to be careful when they explained about the rival high school in the county to the east. Unbeknownst to Aria and Joel, the rivalry between the two schools went deeper than football. The only other pack in the western half of Montana was based in the nearby city. The city pack and the Silver Creek pack were long standing rivals because the city pack feared the Silver Creek pack for their extra abilities. The fear came out as aggression if the two packs were around each other for any length of time. For the most part the packs kept to their own territories.

Chapter 2

After everyone left Aria and Joel decided to leave the rest of the unpacking for tomorrow. They both collapsed onto their newly made beds. Aria lay awake thinking of her mother, her aunt, her new house, and of the sexy Xavier.

A couple of short hours later, Xavier waited impatiently in the guest house, where he and Gage lived, for Gabriel's headlights to shine through the window. He had been pacing all night. Gage had growled at him to stop. When it became likely the two were going to get into a fight Gage opted to go to bed early over wrestling with his roommate.

Finally, the lights he'd been waiting for shone through the window. Xavier was outside the door and next to Gabriel's truck before he had even put it in park.

"Katrina told me you were waiting." Gabriel said as he opened the door. "A bit impatient, aren't you?"

"I haven't been waiting patiently either," Katrina admitted coming up the walk to meet them.

"I'm sorry. I'm just so curious. What is preventing her from shifting?" Xavier began, "She smells like a wolf, she smells of the extra that Kiera and you have." Xavier pointed at Katrina, "But I can tell she hasn't changed."

Gabriel and Katrina exchanged a look. Neither one of them realized that Xavier could smell the extra.

"Let's go inside and talk." Gabriel wrapped his arm around his wife and held out his hand for Xavier to follow.

"Xavier, you know about our wolf heritage. We teach all of you pups about our other half, so you know how to control it, embrace it, and live with it. You know that most of our male wolves are born with an extra ability to shift into a grizzly bear." Gabriel began and looked at Katrina.

"But my mother, Cheri," Katrina continued, "was born with abilities far beyond that of most shapeshifters. As far as we know she was the first in over 2 generations to be born with "the witch gift".

"Obviously, I've heard the rumors, but you all keep pretty quiet about it." Xavier looked at them waiting for more.

Gabriel's stomach tightened; his greatest fear was that something would happen to Katrina or Kiera because of the witch gift. He figured it ran strong in Kiera's blood. Her eyes held a deep wild in them that was hard to fathom. He hadn't seen Aria, but he had grown up with Cassie and other females in the pack that possessed the witch gift. They all had something extra, something special, most other shifters could tell by meeting them that they were different. But after what happened to Tessa and Cassie, Katrina's mother, Cheri, had made sure the scent of a witch born could be hidden. He thought Xavier himself possessed something extra. Since he could sense Kiera's otherness despite the cloaking spell. It would make sense since Xavier's mother, Tessa, was witch born. He wondered if anyone else could tell. He shook himself breaking that thought before he got lost in it. He looked at Katrina and nodded.

"How much do you know about what happened the night Tessa and Cassie had the incident that led to Cassie leaving and Tessa," Katrina paused.

"It's alright Katrina, you can say Tessa's death" Xavier sighed.

"Yes" Katrina did not want to hurt Xavier by reminding him of his young mother who had died that night when Xavier himself had been only two months old.

"Katrina, you know I don't know much, none of you will even speak of my father." Xavier was starting to feel the frustration he always felt when the topic of his father arose.

"The events of that night happened in part because of the witch gift." Katrina started.

"The witch gift?" Xavier looked shocked. "Katrina, you mentioned it earlier, but I thought," he stuttered… "I thought you were going to tell me it was just rumors."

"No, but this was, is, a well-kept secret, when Cassie and I were born my mother knew immediately that we had been born with the gift. Living here so close to a rival pack we could not let anyone know we possessed the gift."

Xavier interrupted her, speaking only one word that chilled her to the core, "Kiera?"

Before Katrina could even blink Gabriel pinned Xavier to the back of the couch, "Don't you ever breathe that again."

Xavier locked eyes with him. "I love her like my own sister. I would never betray her."

Gabriel relaxed seeing the truth in his eyes. "I would have eventually had to tell you. As alpha, protecting our pack is important; protecting our witch born is vitally important."

Katrina relaxed as Gabriel retreated. "There was another wolf born with 'the witch gift.'"

Xavier looked at them, "Tessa."

Katrina nodded. "Tessa was born a year and a half after Cassie and me. The first time my mother saw her, she knew Tessa had it as well."

Katrina did not like the next part, "You know your mother got pregnant with you when she was 15 and had you when she was 16. But what you don't know is Cassie and Tessa had been practicing their witch gift. I was too scared to delve into it too deeply, but I did learn some." Katrina sighed, "My mother had taught us mostly self-defense spells."

He knew something had been different about his young mother, but he hadn't known for sure that it had been the witch gift.

"Katrina, you've always avoided this subject and now I know why. It explains so much, even the gift the males of this pack have."

Katrina nodded, "what is left of us elders do believe that the ability of most of our male wolves to also shift to the great brown bear is a result of the witch gift. A long time ago when our European ancestors left Ireland, they traveled through eastern Europe. They mingled with travelers; many called them gypsies. When we came through the great cold expanse and dropped down into this region, we mingled with the native people here as well. Our Pack grew strong and many of our gifts began to emerge. It wasn't until other packs started to migrate directly from Europe that our gifts were seen as a bad thing." Katrina laughed without humor. "Imagine werewolves being superstitious about other gifts."

Xavier smiled at her and rolled his eyes, "Yeah, that doesn't make much sense."

Katrina shook her head and continued. "So other packs know our male wolves can shift to the brown bear as well, that has become accepted. Which has been helpful, because it makes other packs think twice before attacking us." She paused, gathering her resolve, "what is not well known is that some of our females possess the ability to practice magic. Tessa and Cassie embraced their magic and became particularly good at it. Unfortunately, Tessa and Cassie were also young teenage girls who fell in love with two pups associated with the Missoula pack, Evan and Tom. I do believe Evan was in love with Cassie, but Tom was just a good actor. Within months Tessa had completely changed, she was a shell of herself, and she was pregnant. Over the next nine months your grandparents tried to separate your mother from Tom, but she kept defying them and sneaking out to see him. Then you were born, and we all loved you. Evan was starting to pull away from his pack and stay at our house more and more. Finally, your mother started to wake up. Her love for you broke through Tom's hold. She realized

Tom would eventually abuse both of you, and she would have never let anyone hurt you. The night of mine and Cassie's senior prom changed everything. You were two months old, and we convinced your mother to come to our prom." Katrina smiled remembering, "Your mother was Gabriel's date, she looked beautiful in her satin cream dress with emerald beads on it. Sophomores weren't allowed to go unless they went with an upperclassman, so we went as a group of 5 determined not to make your mother feel like a fifth wheel. Evan received a phone call that caused him and Cassie to argue, Evan left, and Cassie was so upset she decided to leave as well. Tessa went with her. My parents had gone out to your grandparents' house. With everyone out that night Tessa and Cassie went home to our empty house. Tom was there waiting for them with some other young men from the Missoula pack. Evan must have betrayed Cassie and Tessa to Tom. "They…" She paused uncomfortable to describe the young men's motives and actions to Xavier.

"It's alright Katrina." Xavier said. "I know what they did to my mom."

Katrina looked at him, "They grabbed Tessa and Tom beat her while the others went after Cassie who had run. I think they must have thought Cassie ran away from fear, but Cassie would have never abandoned Tessa. Cassie came back with a spell and a potion, but she was too late, Tom had already injured your mother too severely. Cassie lost it. Her anger fueled whatever spell she was going to use that night and well, the truth is Xavier I don't know." Katrina sighed. "She called me and said, 'Trina get Dad and the guard. Tom and 5 others are here. They have Tessa, I'm not waiting.' And she hung up. When we all got there, there was blood from at least 8 different wolves including Cassie and Tessa. Cassie was clinging to Tessa's body screaming. I will never forget it when I saw my twin; in a ruined sunshine yellow gown streaked with red, her eyes were glowing while an eerie light dripped from her. Her fiery red hair was floating on a calm night. I ran to her and held her, it stopped her from screaming but then she kept repeating 'I'm sorry, I was too late,' over and over. My dad had Gabriel pick her up and move her away from Tessa's body. We could all see she wasn't ready to talk. Tessa was gone. We all howled with rage and anguish. Gabriel gave Cassie to our dad who brought her inside. We still have no idea what happened that night, what spell Cassie used. My mom and I cleaned her up and laid with her until she slept. Dad, Gabriel, and the guard split up. Some stayed to protect you and your grandparents, some stayed to protect us, and some went hunting, but to no avail. No one ever heard from the six, not ever, and by morning Cassie had disappeared."

Xavier sighed, he studied the woman who had raised him for the last three years. He had lived with her since his grandparents had died along with Katrina's parents in a car accident about 13 years after that tragic night. "I had heard some of that before but not all of it. I'm not sure what to think," he looked at her with fear in his eyes. "What if I'm evil like my father?"

Katrina stepped forward. "No. Your father was evil because he chose to be. You may have it somewhere inside of you, I think all wolves do, but you set yourself apart by choosing good."

Gabriel looked into Xavier's eyes. "She's right, you choose who you are, your blood does not control that."

Xavier looked at Katrina, "Did you learn more magic after that?"

"My mother, Natasha, and I studied it until they died." Katrina sighed, "Yes, Gage's mother Natasha. My mother was drawn to Natasha because of her witch blood. We tried to go over what Tessa and Cassie were researching but mostly we were working on a cloaking spell in case more witch born babies or people came into the pack."

"We will get to know Aria and figure out the situation." Katrina said, "We have a lot to figure out."

"Xavier, in a few years I plan to hand this pack over to you and take my place on the elder's council. Your mom was supposed to inherit the alpha title. You will be a young alpha, but the elder's counsel will guide you. You will be charged with protecting the pack, especially our witch born females." Gabriel drew in a breath. "Please do not speak to anyone about this, unless you clear it with me first. You may speak with Gage about it but make sure he understands the importance of keeping this secret."

"I'll keep the secret." Xavier promised, looking directly into Gabriel's eyes. He wasn't challenging Gabriel, he wanted him to see he was sincere. "I really do love Kiera as if she were my own sister." Then Xavier turned to Katrina, "And I love you like my own mother, I would never harm either of you. I will keep my promise as a member of the guard and eventually as alpha to protect this pack."

Katrina smiled at him, tears forming in her eyes, as she rose to hug him. "I know, and we will figure this out."

Gabriel put his arms around both, "We will figure this out."

Chapter 3

The weekend of unpacking and getting settled into their new home went quickly. Aria and Joel felt situated by Monday morning when Joel left, taking their SUV into the city to meet with Northwest Trucking. He was hoping to start work soon. Aria waved her father off and sat on the hand carved log bench next to the front walk waiting for Katrina. Chris, her cousin, told her that her grandfather had made the large sturdy bench from some trees that had fallen during a bad storm. Knowing that little bit of history about the bench made her feel even more at home and connected to the beautiful wood surroundings she was facing.

"Good morning," Katrina smiled warmly at Aria as she rolled down the passenger window. "Are you ready?"

"Ready as I'll ever be." Aria smiled back climbing into the passenger seat.

The ride into town was long, at least 35 minutes. Aria enjoyed the gorgeous scenery, the pines and the brown underbrush with snow tipped mountains jutting up around them. She hadn't passed through town when she and her father had arrived 3 days ago. Since they were busy unpacking and had bought some groceries a few towns over before arriving, they hadn't needed to go into town yet. She had been told there were a couple places to eat, a gas station, hardware store, grocery store, and some specialty shops for tourists. She was excited to see where her mother had grown up. "Did my mom go to school at Silver Creek High?" Aria asked.

"Yes, it's been in this area for a long time, your grandparents went there as well." Katrina answered wondering what exactly Cassie had told her daughter. "Did your mom ever talk about what it was like growing up here?"

"She told me very little, and I wasn't really old enough to think to ask." Aria looked out the window concentrating on the peak of the nearest mountain to take her mind off the tears starting to form in her eyes. "She said something happened and when I was older, she would explain it." Aria took a deep breath. "Dad doesn't know either. I think it hurts him that she didn't trust him enough to tell him, so I don't talk to him about it anymore."

Katrina was dying to ask her niece if the topic of witches and shapeshifters had ever come up, but she didn't think this was exactly the right time, and she didn't want to alienate her niece, or make her think she was crazy. "Your mother was a good woman, and I miss her so much. I think she thought we blamed her for something that was not her fault. Let's get through your high school introduction and we can talk more another time."

Aria looked hopeful, "Will you tell me why she left and never came back?"

"I don't have the answer to that. We can talk later. By the way I forgot to ask; do you have all of your school supplies?" Katrina asked.

"I have a laptop, folders, notebooks, a scientific calculator, and writing stuff." Aria listed off.

"Well, we'll see if there's anything additional you need and give your dad a call before he leaves the city." Katrina suggested as they pulled in front of the old log and stone building. Aria was surprised, she didn't think she had ever seen a school that looked like a gigantic rustic lodge. "Wow," she said out loud.

"Pretty neat school building, isn't it?" Katrina smiled.

"It is definitely not what I was expecting." Aria's eyes were wide as she scanned the building.

"Most people are surprised by it." Katrina grinned, "you'll love the inside as well. Let's go."

Aria looked at the student parking lot as they headed into the building, "Wow that's a lot of trucks."

"Yes, with the weather around here a truck comes in handy. That SUV you have should do fine. If the weather is bad one of the guys can pick you up, and if the weather is really bad school gets canceled."

"Snow days," Aria smiled, "that sounds fun!"

Xavier was walking through the hallway to his next class when he smelled her. Aria thought, Katrina must have taken her to meet the principal, Mr. Carr. He scanned the hall spotting her near the main entrance. Her golden-red hair was braided down her back. She was wearing a dark green sweater, black jeans, and black fashion boots. Her coat was draped over her arm, and she looked amazing. He saw Andrew looking at her and was surprised by the depth of jealousy that ran through him. "Mine," his wolf growled. The brown bear in him was always buried deeper, rarely showing itself. The wolf in him was much more pronounced but he even felt the brown bear rise up to attack at the sight of another male looking at his mate with lust. Whoa, that stopped him dead. He'd been thinking of her all weekend, but mate. He really was losing his mind. He shook his head to clear it and purposely turned away from her to get to his next class.

Aria thought the day had been fun. After meeting her new principal, Katrina had taken her to lunch and showed her some of the shops around town. Then they had picked up Kiera so the three of them could go to dinner. Aria loved her cousin and could tell they would be close. When Joel got back, she learned he was going to start work in two days. She was going to start school the same day. She and her father decided to go shopping to get the furniture and other necessities they needed for their new home. Joel wanted to make sure Aria was all settled before he left. He also insisted that they needed a good food supply in case his daughter was snowed in.

Her first day of school had been a success. She had met a lot of new people and a few people who she thought didn't like her. There was a group of Senior girls that were very cold towards her. Their ringleader was named Kelsey. Aria thought the girl had been fine up until she saw Xavier talking to Aria. Thankfully, most of the other people she meant were nice. Kiera had driven in with her. She was waiting for Kiera now and they were going to go get some things from the shops in town to decorate the house with some local décor. Aria wanted to get some things for her bedroom as well.

"Ready" Kiera asked, opening the passenger side door and getting in.

"Yes," Aria exclaimed. She was excited to get to spend more time with her cousin.

Aria parked her car and the two headed into the first shop on the block that had candles and photographs of the local area. A man was walking by the outside of the shop just minutes after the girls went inside and stopped dead. He could not believe his nose. He had been smelling wolf shifters all over town and was thinking it was lucky he had not encountered one. He knew a strange wolf, who had not introduced himself to the pack's alpha, would not be welcomed. He thought his scent was hidden by the special cologne he was wearing but he didn't want to risk it. His alpha had assured him that there was something extra in the cologne that blocked his scent from other shifters, but he was still worried. He waited on the bench by the front of the store. The wind was blowing towards him. He hoped that they would continue into the wind to the next shop instead of backtracking past him. He was taking a chance, but the she-wolf's scent was so intoxicating he had to take the chance. He thought luck must be on his side when the two females exited and headed into the wind.

A couple hours later, Aria dropped Kiera off and drove home. She enjoyed her time with Kiera. Aria got candles, local photography in rustic frames, books, and some pottery. Best of all she had made plans for Kiera to sleep over on Friday night. She was feeling really happy when she dropped off Kiera. Katrina was going to pick her up a bit later for dinner.

On her way home she decided she wanted a fire when she got home from eating dinner at Katrina's and Kiera's. She wanted to get everything ready, so she could snuggle up with a fire and the new book she had found in town. She got her old coat on and went out to get wood to fill the wood box. As she approached the woodshed she looked around at the amazing view. She saw what looked like a path and, distracted by the beauty around her decided to follow it for a while.

As she walked, she took in her surroundings. The brush was turning brown, but it was still full from summer growth. The lodgepole pines were towering over her as she walked through them. The air smelled like fall. She was pleasantly surprised that she recognized autumn's scent in her new home thousands of miles away from her old one. She couldn't get over the view of the majestic white tipped mountains in the distance. She walked further down the path then she had intended, lost in the awe of her surroundings. When she realized she had followed the path further into the woods then she had meant to she felt fear. When she turned to head back, she could no longer make out the path. She must have gone off the path without realizing it.

She pulled her cell out of her pocket. "AHHHHH!" she screamed when she saw there was no signal.

"How could I be so stupid?" she chided herself out loud. Her father had been gone a day and she had already gotten herself in trouble. "Great, now he'll never trust me." She told the forest. She debated on what she should do next. They always say if you're lost you should stay in one place, but that advice assumed someone would come to find her. No one knew she had gone for a walk. No one knew to look for her. Katrina had promised Joel she would come get her for dinner this first night she was on her own, but she didn't know what time Katrina was coming. Aria decided to walk towards a clearing she could see to her west. She had only taken 3 steps when she stepped wrong on a rock and fell. She fell hard on her back. She lay there assessing her body. Her back was a bit sore from impact with the ground, but she was more concerned about the pain in her ankle. She swore out loud as she sat up to look at her injury. Dejected, she sat there staring at her ankle.

He had seen the two girls in town pulling out of a parking spot and had nearly hit the car in front of him. They were both beautiful, striking and exactly what his alpha was looking for. He knew there was a local pack in town and had wondered if the girls were wolves. After the girls had left the candle shop, he had gone in to familiarize himself with their scents. One of them smelled like wild, untamed woods and the other smelled like a normal human girl. He had never smelled a more primal scent and thought whichever girl smelled of the wild must be special. He pulled up in front of the log house awhile after Aria had walked into the woods. As he was knocking on the door, he had decided to say he was a salesman but there was no answer. He faintly smelled the wild scent, but it was not enough to indicate that that girl lived there. This must be where the other one lived, he thought. He poked around the house and outbuildings looking for a stronger indicator of the wild scent. When he didn't find it, he got back in his car and left, assuming from the lack of movement that not even the normal girl was there.

When Katrina got out of her truck at Aria's the smell hit her like a slap in the face. A strange wolf had been there. "Aria" she screamed out loud panicking for a moment. She ran towards the house, her pulse racing so fast she felt dizzy. She pushed open the front door. "Aria," she screamed again. When there was no sign of her, she grabbed her cell phone, almost dropping it, her hands were shaking so badly, "Gabriel."

"What's wrong Kitty?" Gabriel asked, hearing the fear in her voice when she said his name.

"Aria is gone and there was a strange wolf here, come quick." Katrina was yelling.

"Be careful," Gabriel commanded and hung up. By the time Gabriel, Gage, Brian, Chris, and Xavier came out of the forest Katrina was certain that the strange wolf had not left with Aria.

"What happened?" Gabriel asked once he'd changed back to human form.

"I smelled the stranger and panicked, I'm sorry." Katrina stepped into Gabriel who held out his arms to comfort her. Katrina was strong and was not quick to panic but the thought of losing her sister's child when she had just found her had made her momentarily lose it.

"I smell him too," Gabriel rubbed his hands up and down Katrina's back soothing her. Gage, Brian, Chris, and Xavier were all still in wolf form, their hackles raised at the stranger's scent, unwelcome in their territory. "He did not leave with her." Gabriel confirmed. At this confirmation Xavier yipped and took off following Aria's scent trail. He had found it leading into the woods by the woodshed. Gabriel started to turn towards Xavier becoming his wolf before he made it to the line of trees encroaching on the yard.

"Remember she doesn't know," Katrina called after them.

Aria was sitting thinking about the coming dark, and she was beginning to get afraid again. The forest had called to her and seemed comforting earlier. But as the shadows grew, the joy it had brought her began to fade.

Xavier stopped when he could tell by the changing scent trail, he was close. He looked at Gabriel, silently asking for permission. Gabriel nodded and he and Brian turned back towards the house.

Chris had stayed behind with Katrina at Aria's house in case the strange wolf returned. There was no way Gabriel was leaving Katrina alone. He had left Drew and Blake, who had been over playing video games with Chris, behind with Kiera. They had already sent out a group text to warn everyone in the pack there was a stranger in town.

Xavier stopped, backtracked a bit, and shifted back to human when Aria's scent grew strong. He began yelling "Aria!"

Aria jumped, was that her name or was the forest playing tricks on her? "Hello!" She yelled.

Xavier moved closer towards her, "Aria!" He called out again.

She got up and started to stumble towards his voice, her ankle protesting. "I'm here" she yelled as she broke through a thick patch of brush under the lodgepole pines.

"There you are!" Xavier exclaimed, pretending he had just found her. "We have been worried sick, what are you doing out here?" He asked, crossing his arms over his chest and looking down at her like she was an errant child.

"Don't look at me like that." Aria said, straightening up. "I went for a walk and got lost." She glared at him. "It could happen to anyone."

"No, cause most people don't wander around the woods by themselves without knowing where they're going." Xavier admonished.

Aria rolled her eyes at him, "Obviously I thought I knew where I was going." Now she hoped he knew where he was going so, she could get home and ice her twisted ankle. She figured he must since he had found her.

"You have got to be more careful; you didn't even tell anyone you were going for a walk. We had to guess you would be somewhere out here." Xavier wanted to yell at her, pick her up and carry her back to the house. He could not believe she had been so foolish. "Katrina arrived and found the house empty with your car still there and got very worried."

"I didn't mean to worry anyone." Aria felt bad about worrying her aunt, but Xavier was just ticking her off. "Look, I realize I just moved here from Philadelphia, but I lived in upstate New York for most of my life, my mother loved camping, and she taught me a lot."

Xavier looked at her, "How many grizzly bears are in Upstate New York? How many mountain lions are in upstate New York?" derision in his every word. He heard himself being harsh but couldn't seem to stop.

"Well," Aria started, then stopped and gathered herself. "Why are you being such a jerk?" She was beginning to rethink her positive opinion of Xavier, looks aren't everything.

Xavier took pity on her, "Okay, maybe I'm being a little rough on you." He looked at her realizing that she had no idea that a strange wolf had been at her house causing them all to panic more than if she had just wandered off with the grizzly bears and mountain lions. Hell, he thought she didn't even know shape shifting wolves existed. "Why are you limping?"

"I twisted my ankle, but it'll be fine." She said hastily continuing to limp ahead even though Xavier had stopped.

"Come on," he said, crouching a little, "I'll give you a piggyback ride, you look exhausted." He didn't want the first time they were alone together to be him just yelling at her.

She hesitated, "Are you sure you can carry me that far?"

"Oh, please. You're a tiny little thing." He gave her a wry smile, "plus I actually do camp in the woods, in remote areas, carrying backpacks heavier than you."

She wanted to say well, aren't you special, but instead Aria weighed how far the walk back might be with the pain in her ankle and decided to just go with it and climbed on his back. "If I get too heavy, let me know." He snorted and began to walk.

As they made their way through the woods, Xavier seemed to glide through the underbrush that was turning crisp, as the forest started to hibernate for the coming winter. He never lost his footing despite his burden. "I didn't mean to scare anyone." Aria blurted out after spending most of the way back in silence trying to decide what she thought of Xavier.

Xavier wished he could explain why everyone was so worried, but he had no idea how to explain it all to her, and he didn't think she would believe him anyway.

Xavier broke through the trees and into the clearing by the house. "Aria!" Katrina exclaimed with relief in her voice and ran to the two of them as Xavier let Aria gently down on her injured ankle.

"What happened?" Katrina asked, bracing Aria's other side as she stumbled a bit.

"I'm fine, I just lost my footing and twisted my ankle a bit. I went for a walk and next thing I knew I had lost the path and had no idea where I was." Aria looked at her aunt. "I'm so sorry. It's so beautiful out here. I was busy staring around and got lost, I didn't mean to make everyone worry."

Katrina knew that Aria had no idea why they'd all been so worried. If Katrina had arrived to find her missing without the scent of the strange wolf, yes, she would have been worried. The mountains held moose, mountain lions, and bears both black and brown, but she would not have felt that instant panic that hit her when she had smelled the unknown wolf.

Aria watched a tall man with black hair and dark eyes approach them. The man had a presence like Xavier, and before she could speak, he said, "I'm Gabriel, Katrina's husband. We overreacted. There are a lot of animals in these woods that are looking to fatten themselves up before winter comes. You're more than welcome to hike but until you learn how to shoot or at least get some bear spray it may be better if you hike with someone."

Katrina smiled at Gabriel and then turned back to Aria. "He's right, I was so scared when you weren't here that I overreacted." Katrina eyed her again, "are you sure you're alright?"

"I'm just tired and a bit sore; I was scared too once I realized I was lost. Xavier found me shortly after, really, nothing to worry about." Aria's expression was certain.

"Alright, then let's go get some food." Katrina kept her arm around Aria's back helping her to the SUV. She exchanged a look with Gabriel over Aria's head. The others were just out of sight, so Aria never knew they were there. Katrina knew that Gabriel wanted to stay behind to look over everything and figure out where the strange new wolf had been on the property so she didn't act surprised when he said, "We'll fill up your firewood boxes and be right behind you." as Katrina and Aria got into the car.

As soon as they pulled away Gage, Brian, and Chris stepped out of the woods. "What are we going to do?" Gage asked.

"She needs protection," Xavier said.

"Yes," Gabriel, looked at them, "all pack members will need to be on high alert. I want you to call or text all pack members and set up a meeting for tonight at 9 PM." He looked at Xavier "I want you to offer to bring her home, you can feel out the situation and stay with her inside, if she seems uncomfortable, stay outside. Someone will relieve you at 2am so you can get some sleep."

Xavier wanted to say he would stay till morning but knew he was no good to Aria or his pack if he was exhausted. "Will do."

Gabriel nodded, sensing that Xavier was attracted to Aria, and proud that he had made the smart decision, not insisting he do everything alone. "Let's figure out where our unwelcome visitor went."

They all split up and began sniffing around in different locations, realizing the stranger appeared to have just looked around and left.

Satisfied Gabriel directed Brian, "Stay here until Xavier and Aria get back."

Brian nodded, "I'll call if anyone shows up."

Gabriel nodded and hugged his son, "Call immediately and do not engage the new wolf on your own." Gabriel worried about Brian, he could fight but Brian was a healer by nature and often hesitated in a fight.

Brian looked at Gabriel, "Dad" he complained.

Gabriel ruffled Brian's hair "Just call." Everyone else started to shift to run back to Gabriel's house. Before he changed Gage turned to Brian, "I'm going to be the Beta; the pack's lead fighter, and I would call for backup."

"Yeah right," Brian called after Gage as he changed to a large black wolf and disappeared into the forest.

"Go get Aria settled at the table, get her something to drink, and some ice for her ankle. She's exhausted." Katrina told Kiera as soon as they walked in the house.

Kiera grinned at Aria. "Right this way, clumsy Dora the Explorer."

Aria rolled her eyes at her cousin's cheerful grin and followed her to the kitchen.

They had a nice dinner. Joel had told Katrina that Aria loved chicken pot pies, so Katrina had made them for dinner hoping to make Aria feel at home and welcome. After dinner Aria sat around and told stories about camping with her mom followed by Katrina telling Aria heavily edited stories about camping with Cassie when they were young. Katrina found it difficult to share stories about her twin and leave out the fact they were constantly shifting in and out of wolf form.

As discussed, Xavier volunteered to bring Aria home. "Thanks for the ride." Aria said as she climbed out of Xavier's truck.

"Do you want me to help you get a fire started? I see you're walking on that ankle better, but you may want to keep resting it tonight so it's better by morning." Xavier asked.

Joel had bought Aria fire starters, matches, and had cut her some kindling so she thought she could probably get the fire going but decided it would be nice to spend some time with Xavier when he wasn't scolding her and carrying her out of the woods like a damsel in distress. "Sure, that'd be nice," she said.

He shut off the truck and went inside with her. He asked her about her day while he got the fire going. They talked for a bit, but Xavier got the impression she was tired, so he bid her goodnight. He got into his truck and drove it down the road and out of sight of the house. He shifted into his wolf and ran back to the edge of the yard settling down to watch the house for any sign of the other wolf returning.

Aria got ready for bed analyzing Xavier's every word. He had kind of been a jerk in the woods, but he was really nice the rest of the night. He had even started a fire for her and talked for a while. She hoped she didn't sound like an idiot blathering about her classes and how much she enjoyed the view of the surrounding area. She dwelled on Xavier as she brushed her teeth, washed her face, and put on her pajamas. She fell asleep still thinking over her night with him and feeling right at home.

Chapter 4

The strange wolf's name was Glen. He was from a pack, currently residing in Northern Siberia, that often "recruited" females. The pack's Alpha was from the states and had a habit of making female wolves disappear. When the female population started to decline his Alpha would send trusted pack members out to "recruit". The Alpha's idea of "recruiting" was to kidnap the females and force them to join his pack. He thought his Alpha would do better to stop making them disappear so they wouldn't have to risk other packs finding out they had been kidnapping females for over a decade. His Alpha had insisted on looking at the pack in Silver Creek for his next acquisition. He thought his Alpha had been in the states about three years ago, but he had not come back with any females. Glen thought that the she-wolf he had scented would be a fantastic addition to his pack. She smelled strong and capable. She was a bit young, but they could give her to the families that fostered the young females without parents until she was ready to be married off. He hoped the cologne was strong enough to mask his scent until he could figure out where the little, she-wolf lived. He decided he would keep looking and if he couldn't figure it out, he would have to get the human girl to tell him.

When Brian showed up to relieve Xavier from guard duty Xavier was still keyed up. "How was the meeting?"

"It went well, Dad told the whole pack to be on the lookout for a strange wolf." Brian sighed. "We are wondering why no one else could smell him. Dad brought a piece of the shrub the stranger brushed up against so the pack would know who they were looking for and only some of the pack could smell wolf."

"Really?" Xavier's mind began to race.

"Yep," Brian confirmed. "Everyone in our family could smell it. Gage, Jordan, Anna, Elle, and some others could smell it, but no one else."

Xavier immediately knew the connection, everyone with a blood tie to a witch born could smell it. He didn't want to say anything unsure if Gabriel had told Brian about the witch gift. "Strange," Xavier said out loud, not wanting his face to give away his epiphany.

"Dad is going into town with Gage in the morning. They are going to go to the hotel and some of the B&B's and see if they can find where he's staying. The Sheriff is going to search as well."

Xavier was grateful Greg was elected as Sheriff 15 years ago, making everyone's life a lot easier. Most of the deputies were wolves as well, so it made it easier for the pack to maneuver within town. The pack was large since they had always taken in strays. He thought of Gage. Gage's mother had shown up in the nearby city with a young Gage, Cheri had insisted on taking them in. Gage's young mother had emigrated as a teenager from Eastern Europe after leaving her pack. She had run into Cheri at the restaurant she was working in. Gage's mother was killed in the same accident that had killed Xavier's grandparents and Katrina's parents. He thought of the fact that Gage could smell the scent and wondered now if Cheri had insisted on taking Natasha in because she had the witch gift as well. It would make sense since pack legend had insisted that the witch gift started to emerge after his Celtic ancestors passed through Eastern Europe having children with the packs there. Gage had proved very skilled in combat both as a person and a wolf, the council had decided to groom him for the position of Beta. The packs' Beta was always the strongest fighter. The Alpha had to be able to beat the Beta if needed but Xavier thought that in a good pack the challenge would never come, so there would be no need for the Alpha to defend himself or herself against the Beta. Xavier and Gage had been friends since they were two years old, when Cheri had brought Natasha home. After the accident they had moved into a small guest house Gabriel and the pack had built for them next to Katrina and Gabriel's home, so they could have some freedom but also have some supervision as they had still been young teenagers.

"Xavier?" Brian questioned, concerned that Xavier appeared to be off in la la land.

"Sorry," Xavier apologized, bringing his mind back to the present. "I'm just worked up, thanks for relieving me. Hopefully Gage and Gabriel will be able to find the stranger."

Several hours later in town Glen had just finished his breakfast when the door opened at the front of the large old bed and breakfast he was staying at on the western edge of Silver Creek. The wind blew through the door pushing the scent of those who had just entered to the back of the house where he was standing. His heart stopped, he smelled power. He was debating on whether he should go for his things or run out the back door when he heard the hostess walking to the front of the house, "Good Morning, gentlemen." He heard her voice echo back through the house. He made a split decision to run up the backstairs to his room. He grabbed the bag he kept packed for just such an occasion and shimmied out the window. Dropping from the second floor was not hard for a wolf. He hit the ground running. He got in his car and started down the drive. Gabriel and Gage heard the car start as they were speaking with the Bed and Breakfast's owner. They looked out the window in time to see the car disappearing down the driveway.

"Damn" Gabriel sighed in frustration.

"I can't believe it," Gage said.

"What's wrong?" asked Ms. Helen, the owner of the Bed and Breakfast whom they'd been talking to.

"That man was acting kind of strange to some of the high school girls," Gabriel explained. "We were trying to see where he was staying so we could let the Sheriff know."

"Oh my," Ms. Helen said. "I'll let Greg know immediately if he comes back."

"I bet Greg would appreciate any information on him as well." Gabriel suggested.

"I will certainly give him anything he needs." Ms. Helen agreed, "You boys have a good day, I'm going to get his information together and call Greg right away."

The pack hadn't been able to figure out much since the strange wolf had escaped them. Sheriff Greg had tried to run the name he had been given by Ms. Helen but only found a dead end. The pack continued to stay on alert and although she didn't know it Aria was never alone. The pack took turns watching her house ensuring she was safe. Even when Joel was home the pack watched over them both. They were part of the pack whether they knew it or not and they would not leave helpless pack members without protection. As the weeks passed, they did not relax the pack restrictions, making sure no pack member was out alone. Gabriel and the council agreed something felt wrong about this wolf, strangers usually did not come into town and stay without asking Gabriel for his permission first.

Aria was excited it was Friday. The last few Fridays' Kiera had come over and spent the night. She had been able to learn all about her cousin and share her life with her cousin as well. On Saturday's she had been going to Kiera's and spending time with her aunt and the rest of the family. Katrina would send the guys over to do any chores Aria needed like refilling the wood boxes, raking leaves, changing light bulbs, or chopping wood. Joel would spend a day or two at home when he could. She thought the last couple weeks in Montana had been wonderful. Aria stretched and opened her curtain looking out over the vast view of the mountains. She saw it was sleeting and wondered if the roads would be slippery. Kiera, who normally rode to school with her, was riding in early with Gage and her brothers because she had an early meeting with a teacher. Aria decided to take her time and enjoy the morning.

After a leisurely breakfast and getting dressed in her favorite high waisted black jeans and a purple wool sweater she checked out the outfit in the mirror. She had been watching one of her favorite YouTube channels, Hannahleedugan, and wanted to dress like Hannah. She looked at the clock and realized she had taken too much time. She would be late if she didn't hurry. She decided her outfit would be fine, grabbed her backpack, and threw on her shoes and jacket as she ran to the door leading to the attached garage. She was lucky she parked in the garage, so she did not have to scrape ice off her car. As she backed out of the garage her back tires fishtailed a bit, so she slowed down. Seeing her back out of the garage Xavier uncurled from his watch place and took off running towards home. He had to get into his own truck and make it to school. He figured that he would catch her no problem since it appeared she was driving slowly.

She started down the long driveway at a slow pace. By the time she got to the shared part of the drive that led down to the main road she thought she was starting to get the hang of this icy driving thing. Unfortunately, about 100 yards later an elk ran in front of her car startling her. The elk hadn't been close enough to hit but it made her tense and started her heart racing. When the second elk ran out, she swerved instead of staying on the road and her SUV slid off the main driveway and since the ground had not frozen, yet her SUV sunk into the muddy earth alongside the road.

"Perfect," she said out loud to herself. She tried to move the vehicle back and forth a bit but thought she was just sinking further into the mud. She looked around and realized she had forgotten her phone in her haste to get out of the house. She got out of her vehicle and surveyed the situation. She decided instead of sitting here feeling sorry for herself while she got drenched in a cold icy sleet, she had better start walking back to her house to call Katrina and Gabriel.

Xavier missed Aria by seconds. She had just started up the portion of driveway that led to her house when Xavier got to the part where the two driveways merged. It didn't take him long to come across the SUV. He jumped out a little worried and started looking around. He saw there was no sign of blood. He found Aria's tracks leading back towards the houses. He could still smell the Elk in the air and figured she had swerved to avoid hitting one. He turned his truck around and started back up the drive, this time turning towards Aria's house instead of his own. He found her around the first bend.

"You lost again?" He said, rolling down his window as he pulled alongside her.

She glared at him, "Not funny, I do NOT need to be rescued." she drew out the word 'not' making sure he heard it.

"I thought it was being neighborly to offer a ride." Xavier replied. "Though it appears your vehicle needs to be recused."

"Stupid Elk." Aria muttered.

"Get in the truck." Xavier said.

She stuck her nose in the air, "I'm fine, thank you."

He rolled his eyes, damn she was stubborn. "Get in the truck Aria. There is no need to continue getting cold and wet."

She finally stopped and looked at him. "Fine." She marched around the front of the truck and climbed in. He turned the heat on high, she was drenched and shivering. He kept going back up the drive, putting the truck in park when he pulled in front of her house.

"I'll call Gabriel while I wait. If you hurry, we may make it to school just in time." Xavier told her as he pulled out his cell.

"Wait, what am I doing?" Aria asked.

"Well, I assumed you didn't want to go through school soaking wet and cold." Xavier pointed out. "I also assumed you would want your vehicle pulled out and you would want to get to school."

Aria sighed, starting to climb out of the truck, saying "Well, I guess you didn't make an ass out of yourself this time." And she shut the door.

He laughed out loud, guessing that meant his assumption was right.

Aria quickly changed into brown corduroys and a burnt orange sweater. She grabbed her cell phone off the counter on her way back out to the truck. "Gabriel will get it pulled out before the end of the day." Xavier told her as she climbed back in the passenger's seat.

"Thank you," Aria sighed, "Can we please stop and grab my backpack and purse?"

"Absolutely." Xavier smiled.

They were almost to the school when Xavier asked. "Are you and Kiera going to the party tonight?"

"Yep, we're going with Anna, and Ellie." Aria said. "I'm excited. Kiera says the Halloween bonfire parties are a lot of fun!"

"They are." Xavier confirmed.

"Are you and the guys going?" Aria asked.

"Yes, we'll be a bit later as we promised Gage, we would go with him to look at a truck for sale, his truck is having problems." Xavier explained.

"That's nice of you." Aria was excited that Xavier was going to be at the party but didn't want to sound overly eager.

"Thanks for the ride." Aria said climbing out of his truck once they got to the school. "I'll ride home with Ellie. She was going to come to my house right after school anyway."

Aria, Kiera, Anna, and Ellie got ready for the party at Aria's house. Kiera had bought them all black cotton yoga pants with black sweatshirts that had pumpkins and candy corns all over them. She thought it would be fun to dress up a bit but none of them had wanted to wear actual costumes. Kiera always ordered 100% natural clothes when she could because synthetic materials did not shift with her when she became a wolf. The girls planned on meeting some other friends at the park where the party was so after they grabbed some food and finished getting dressed, they headed to the park. When the girls arrived, Aria was surprised to see how many of their classmates were already there. "I'm going to go see if Kristen is here yet." Aria told Kiera after they'd met up with Becca.

"Alright we're going to wait here for Lindsay, and we'll meet you up by the bridge. It may end up being 20-30 minutes knowing Lindsay." Kiera laughed and told Aria.

"Alright Kristen texted and said she's up there with Kelsey and some other girls. Are you sure you're alright with me going ahead?"

"Yes, I don't expect a junior to only hang out with sophomores." Kiera grinned at her.

Aria grinned and called back "Well you all better hurry because I like hanging out with sophomore's," as she disappeared down the dark path that led up to the bridge. Kiera had told her there were always three bonfires. One near the entrance of the park, one up by the bridge that crossed the river, and the other over by the beach where the river was dammed and made an artificial lake.

Chapter 5

It had been awhile since Aria left to go up to the bridge, Kiera kept checking her watch as she waited for Lindsay. "Did you guys hear Kelsey dare the new girl to walk to the waterfall and back?" Kiera overheard one of the juniors asking as she was walking up to the group standing behind Kiera. Kiera stood stock still listening before jumping into the conversation. Her father kept telling her to wait, to listen, to think, before acting. "Well, you know Kelsey has always had a thing for Xavier, and he has had his eye on the new girl since she got here. She's probably hoping a grizzly bear will eat her. Since they're fattening themselves up before hibernation." A blonde-haired junior responded. Kiera didn't need to wait to hear any more. Aria had gone up to the bridge about 25 minutes ago. She could be halfway to the falls by now. She had been catching the scent of a grizzly bear since they had arrived, which with how much noise everyone was making hadn't concerned her, but Aria was alone in the woods.

Kiera turned to her friend, "Anna go get my brothers, Xavier, Gabriel, and any other pack members you can find. They should be in the parking lot or pulling in soon, tell them about the dare." Kiera turned to leave.

Anna grabbed her arm. "Kiera even you can't take on a grizzly bear." Anna exclaimed, biting her lower lip.

``Wanna bet?" With that Kiera turned and ran. When she got to the bridge where the trail to the waterfall crossed the river, a girl stepped in front of her blocking her path.

"Where do you think you're going?" Kelsey glared at Kiera knowing by Kiera's demeanor she had heard her cousin was alone in the woods. "Your cousin accepted the dare, and the dare was she goes alone."

Kiera paused briefly, accessing the stuck up overdone doll that was Kelsey. "You have 2 seconds to get the hell out of my way or I will move you." Kiera warned.

Kelsey didn't know what Kiera was. The pack's children went out of their way to get along with the people in Silver Creek who were not shapeshifters. About half of the community was pack, and half of it was regular people. The pack sometimes married regular people. They did let their spouses in on the secret, mainly because all children resulting from a union between a shifter and regular human created a shifter child.

Kelsey's shock quickly turned to disbelief, she'd always been cordial with Kiera because the stupid little sophomore seemed so important to Xavier, Gabriel, and the other guys that hung out with them. But she was a tiny little bug and had no right speaking to her that way.

"You." Kelsey did not get anything else out before Kiera grabbed her, pulled her forward and wrapping her foot around Kelsey's leg shoved her out of the way as she fell to the forest floor. She heard Kelsey's cry of rage as she started running as fast as she could on two legs, since she had just caught a fresh wave of grizzly bear scent on the breeze.

Aria was wondering what the hell she had been thinking to choose a dare with the group of girls she had been playing truth or dare with. She had suspected Kelsey didn't like her; Aria had seen the way Kelsey's brown eyes turned green when Xavier paid attention to Aria instead of Kelsey. Her pondering was cut short when she heard something large approaching her through the woods, she stopped and started shining her flashlight all around. She realized she didn't need the flashlight, the moon was full, the perfect moon for night hunting. It was nearly as bright as day so when the large brown bear stepped onto the path ahead of her, she had no problem seeing it.

Anna ran to the parking lot hoping that Xavier and the guys were already there. Luck was on her side when she made it to the edge and saw two pick-up trucks pulling in and recognized them as belonging to Brian and Xavier. Xavier almost hit her. She was in such a rush to get over to them she ran right in front of his truck. She needed to make sure that she could get help for Keira and Aria. She just hated to think of Keira 's little red wolf taking on a huge grizzly bear. Xavier and Brian saw the panic on her face, they both threw the trucks in park and jumped out, the others guys jumping out behind them. Gage's blood went cold, he was afraid it was Keira, her and Anna were so close. "What's wrong?" Xavier asked, while Gage searched for a smell or something that would indicate what had happened to make Anna so afraid.

"It's Keira and Aria." Anna explained. "Kelsey dared Aria to walk to the falls and she did. Kiera found out after Aria already left. Kiera went after her by herself. She said she'd been smelling grizzly bear's since we got here." Anna took a breath. "I've caught a few faint whiffs, but you know Keira's sense of smell is way better than mine."

Gage and Xavier did not want to wait for the rest, but they knew they needed to get all the information. "Kelsey dared Aria, and she went, and Keira went after her." Xavier clarified.

"Yes, you know that grizzlies are trying to fatten up before the winter. I'm so scared, you guys have to go." Anna finished pointing up the slope where the bridge lay ahead.

They all took off running as fast as they could. When they got to the bridge, they saw Kelsey leaning against the bridge posts, brushing off her clothes. Kelsey stood and tried to grab Xavier's arm as he approached her. He turned on her and for the first time ever Kelsey was afraid of him. Kelsey took several steps back "What the hell were you thinking? You know it's dangerous and you know she's from the East Coast and you know she doesn't understand the dangers." Xavier chastised in a low dangerous voice.

"If my sister or my cousin gets hurt Kelsey, you'll be sorry." Brian spat at her.

Kelsey took another step back; Gage was about to say something as well when they heard the scream. Forgetting Kelsey, they all turned and ran.

Kiera came around a bend and saw Aria backed up against a tree with a snorting grizzly staring at her. "Aria don't move," Kiera whispered.

"Kiera, run." Aria said, too late, the grizzly began to charge.

"Aria don't freak out." Kiera warned leaping in front of Aria changing into a red wolf mid leap. The little red wolf landed snarling in front of the grizzly bear.

Kiera wasn't sure if it was Aria's high-pitched scream or her own snarls that made the bear pause, but she thought by some miracle it did.

Aria was in shock. Her cousin was a wolf, a red wolf, and there was a big brown angry bear. Her head cleared quickly as the grizzly roared at the little red wolf and swiped out its huge paw trying to knock the wolf out of the way. Aria screamed again sure the grizzly would kill the little wolf, the wolf that was Kiera. But Kiera was fast. She was a red blur dodging the paw and landing a nip on the grizzly's sensitive muzzle, quickly retreating before its teeth could close around her. The grizzly was now fully occupied with the little red wolf forgetting about Aria. The two were engaged in a type of combat where the little red wolf would go in close for a nip or swipe at the bear's sensitive face area and the bear would bellow trying to swipe out at the little red wolf to stop the attacks. Aria was shaking from fear she didn't know what she could do to help the little wolf, surely it would not be able to fend off the grizzly for long. The grizzly finally managed to land a blow on the little wolf knocking her into a tree. The grizzly paused blood running down its face where the red wolf had injured it.

When the bear started toward the wolf, Aria's body convulsed. Kiera, little wild Kiera, who was now the little red wolf, was about to be mauled by this huge brown grizzly bear. Without thinking Aria lunged forward to protect Kiera. Mid lunge Aria shifted into a golden red wolf. She stumbled forward, not prepared to have four paws instead of two feet. The commotion distracted the bear. As it turned towards her thousands of years of instinct coursed through her veins and she snarled. She was in her own mind but there was extra. She instinctively moved between the bear and Kiera snarling again. Kiera was beginning to wake up. Kiera yipped in surprise. She knew the wolf standing between her and the bear was Aria because the beautiful golden red wolf smelled like Aria. Kiera stumbled to her feet feeling that some of her ribs were broken knowing it didn't matter, she needed to be on her feet next to Aria. This bear needed to decide they were not worth the fight, they were not food.

Xavier, Gage, Brian, Chris, Blake, and Drew rounded the bend. They saw two wolves, a small golden red wolf and an even smaller red wolf facing off with an extremely large brown bear bellowing at them. The pack had a game plan all set for threats. Xavier and Gage leapt forward turning into brown bears while Brian, Chris, Blake, and Drew leapt forward turning into wolves. All of them snarling and growling at the same time. The enraged bear turned at the sound and charged Xavier and Gage. The two bellowed and met the bear's attack. The four wolves surrounded the wolves that were Aria and Kiera keeping them safe. The huge wild bear fought with Xavier and Gage who were slightly smaller bears. After only minutes the wild bear turned and ran, deciding the threat was too great. Xavier and Gage looked at each other. They could not let a wounded bear roam the woods with a bunch of high school students out partying. Xavier nodded at Gage. Gage shifted quickly. "Are you alright?" He asked Kiera. She met his eyes and nodded. He turned towards Brian "Get them back to the trucks and call your dad, tell him what happened and that we're hunting the wounded bear." He shifted back and the two took off after the wounded wild bear. Xavier took one last look at the golden red wolf who he knew was Aria by her scent.

The four guys and Kiera shifted. Brian ran to Kiera to access her injuries. "I'm okay," Kiera said. "Help Aria." Kiera was breathing heavily but she was not bleeding anywhere. That scared him more as he worried about internal injuries. Brian was going to be a doctor so he could take care of his pack. He had been taking extra courses since he started high school. He tried to inspect her torso, but she yelled at him again, "help Aria." Brian finally heard her and turned towards Aria who was shaking and looking around in panic.

Aria's thoughts were running rampant. She had just seen her cousins shift into wolves, she had just shifted into a wolf and Xavier and Gage had just shifted into bears. She was confused and scared for Xavier and Gage who had just ran after an exceptionally large angry bear. But her most pressing matter was that she was a wolf and had no idea how to shift back to a human. She didn't even know if she could shift back but she thought if she saw Kera shift back she could. Brian realized Aria's problem. He stepped towards her "Aria." He kept his tone low and quiet. "Take a deep breath."

Aria was beginning to lose control over the fear. Brian could see the panic deepening in her large hazel eyes. "Aria, think about being human."

Brian's voice was barely penetrating through the fear when a deep booming voice caught her attention. "Shift" the voice ordered. Aria recognized the voice as Gabriel. The command shift wound its way through her. Her wolf recognized Gabriel as Alpha. The fear that had a hold of her loosened its grip on her. With Gabriel's presence her wolf allowed the shift back to human. Aria fainted after taking only a single breath with her human lungs.

"Dad, Mom," Brian exclaimed. "Xavier and Gage went after the wounded bear."

Gabriel turned to Katrina. "Is she okay?"

"Dad it's just a broken rib or two, I'm fine" Kiera rolled her eyes.

Gabriel ignored his daughter and looked at Katrina again who was standing up from checking Kiera to go check on Aria. Katrina nodded, "She has a few broken ribs, maybe a few bruises, nothing else, I think." Katrina looked at Aria. "I think she just fainted from shock."

Gabriel nodded. "Brian, Chris, Blake, take them back to the trucks and get them home." He looked at Katrina still speaking to the 3 young men. "There is still an unknown threat out there." He looked around and started walking over to Kiera "Drew let's go help Xavier and Gage." He bent down and kissed his daughter. "Katrina, call in reinforcements when you get to the parking lot and have cell coverage. Send Greg, Ryan, Al, Kyle, and Dan back here to help us, tell them to track as wolves. I want Lee, Sean, Ben, and Mitch at the house until we get back." With that Gabriel and Drew turned towards the woods Drew shifting to wolf while Gabriel shifted to bear.

"I'll carry her." Brian nodded towards Aria as his father and pack mates disappeared into the forest.

"I can carry Kiera." Chris told his brother moving towards his sister.

"You will not." Kiera said indignantly, standing up slowly.

Everyone looked at Katrina. "Kiera, give before you fall." Kiera looked at her mother and sighed in defeat. With that Chris picked up his sister.

Katrina helped get Aria situated in Brian's arms and they began to walk back towards the river. Katrina walking alongside her children was grateful they were alright. She was still afraid for her husband and her other children out hunting the bear. She might not have given birth to Xavier and Gage, but they were hers now too. "How did you know to come?" asked Brian looking at his mother.

Chapter 6

Katrina didn't know how to explain the rush of sheer terror she had suddenly felt. She had also felt terror the nights Tessa, Cassie, and her parents had died, but it had not been as quite as strong. "Your father and I were sitting watching TV and suddenly I was panicking. All I could think of was I needed to get to my baby girl. Then your father started to feel fear from the pack. We knew where you all were, so we came. Then when we got to the parking lot, Anna was there, and she explained what was happening. We tracked you until we found you."

When they started to cross the bridge Anna and some other young pack members were on the other side waiting for them.

Anna looked so worried, "We're all going to be alright." Katrina shouted ahead of them.

Anna looked relieved. "Everyone left after you and Gabriel came through."

"Let's get to the trucks," Katrina said looking around. She wasn't sure if she was just worried about her family or if it was her intuition telling her to stay alert, but she wanted to get them all to the trucks and out of the area.

After everyone was safe inside the vehicles and starting to move towards the exit, Katrina called everyone. Once the pack was moving into position, she called Jack. Jack was in his early sixties and was the current pack physician. Brian was training to take his place. With Jack's agreement to meet them at the house Katrina relaxed back into her seat stroking Aria's hair with one hand and holding Kiera's hand with her other. Brian was driving and Katrina began to relax her body hoping her daughter and niece would feel it and instinctively relax as well. When a thought suddenly hit her, Aria now smelled similar to Kiera but slightly different. Kiera's scent smelled of the wilds like ancient untouched wilderness where the trees themselves had eyes and those disturbing them would meet an unpleasant end. Aria smelled of ancient wilds as well but also of ancient wisdom. Katrina couldn't quite put her finger on it, but she thought of spirit quests and ancient rituals when she breathed in Aria's scent as opposed to the ancient battle smell that wound through Kiera's scent. Whatever had happened in the clearing had broken Cassie's powerful binding spell.

"Mom, what's wrong?" Kiera asked, nervous when her mother's relaxing body suddenly became rigid.

"It's nothing, baby, just relax; Doc Jack will meet us at the house. He will be able to bind your ribs and give you something for the pain. You should be all good within a day or two." Katrina gave her hand a reassuring squeeze. "Good thing we heal fast, broken ribs hurt!"

"It's Aria, isn't it?" Kiera pressed. "She smells different, strong like me but different."

Katrina sighed. "Not now we'll talk about it once everyone is together, but not now."

Kiera laid her head on her mom's shoulder, "alright."

Doc Jack had looked Kiera over and wrapped her ribs. As a shifter she would heal quickly. Doc had told Katrina that Aria should wake soon and to call him if more than a couple hours passed and she hadn't.

Katrina, Kiera, Brian, and Chris jumped up from where they had been sitting and ran to the door when they heard trucks approaching. They had been on edge fearing for the safety of their pack brothers who had went hunting for the bear.

"We are all fine." Gabriel called to the waiting group as he climbed out of the truck. "Let's get some food and sit down. We'll tell you everything."

While Gabriel and the others were telling them what had happened with the bear Aria woke up.

"What, who, how?" Aria sat up and began to hyperventilate seconds after becoming coherent. Katrina began rubbing her back telling her to take deep breaths.

"Alright," Aria breathed, starting to regain control of her panic, "I'm alright. Can someone please explain what the hell just happened?"

Everyone looked at Gabriel and Katrina. "Kitty?" Gabriel asked, raising his eyebrows.

Katrina nodded and began, "Aria your mother was a shapeshifter and so are you." Katrina paused to see if Aria was going to interrupt. When she stayed silent Katrina continued, "Our ancestors have all been shapeshifters. The females of our pack shift into wolves and some of them are born with magic, we call it the 'witch gift'. The males are born with the ability to shift into both a wolf and some of them a brown bear as well, although the wolf is their primary form." She paused to let her words sink in.

"My mother was a werewolf with magic?" Aria asked.

"Well, we consider ourselves shape shifters, since the moon does not control our shifting, but essentially yes. She left home after a tragic incident, met your father, and had you." Katrina explained. "She used some sort of magic to prevent you from changing and to prevent you from smelling like a wolf. That must have been a powerful spell; even those of the pack with which blood couldn't smell a hint of your true nature."

Aria was shocked, "But tonight." she stopped.

"But tonight, you saw your cousin about to be killed and the spell broke. Your will to protect your cousin was stronger than whatever spell Cassie used." Gabriel finished.

Aria looked at her aunt and uncle, she looked at her cousins, Gage, and Xavier. "My mother never told me. None of you told me."

Kiera looked at her cousin begging her to understand with eyes, "Aria, we didn't know how to tell you. You would have thought we were all nuts."

Aria was beginning to get angry. She stood and began pacing, "I don't know what to think, all of you lied to me." She sucked in a breath when the realization hit her, "My own mother lied to me." she shouted at them.

"Your mother was trying to protect you. We use a spell to muffle Kiera's scent although it is nowhere near as powerful as the one Cassie used for you." Katrina rose and began to approach Aria to soothe her.

Aria held up her hands to stop Katrina from getting any closer. "Does my father know?"

"I doubt it, I think he would have said something." Katrina told her, taking another cautious step closer, yearning to soothe her niece.

"Am I going to turn into a wolf every full moon?" Aria asked, her face going ashen.

"No, we can change at will. No weather pattern or as Katrina mentioned, moon cycle can force a change, but extreme stress can bring on the need to change. It depends on the individual person's control as to whether they actually change under that stress." Gabriel explained.

Aria was relieved but she didn't show Gabriel any emotion. "I'm going home, I need space." Aria said, turning towards the door. Gabriel looked at Xavier. Xavier stood to follow Aria to the door. Aria turned on the room. "I said I need space."

Gabriel stood, he expected Aria to cower, after all she was a teenager, and he was the Alpha. She had no idea what power an Alpha held. "You cannot be left alone." Gabriel decreed. He was surprised when she stood firm, meeting his eyes.

"I don't need a babysitter. I'm not going to tell anyone, but I do need space." Aria said her hazel eyes defiantly meeting Gabriel's dark eyes.

Gabriel smiled to himself. Aria was strong, proud, and held the same stubbornness as her mother and his own wife not to mention his daughter. He should have known with her bloodline she would not be easily swayed by the will of another wolf, even her Alpha. Gabriel never wanted to crush the spirit of those he thought would be running the pack one day, so he knew when to pick his battles and still remain in charge. He wanted to nurture their independence and strength not crush it. "Aria, you are a pack, you are precious to us, we don't think you a traitor." He took a step towards her. "There was a strange wolf at your house a few weeks ago. We think he left because part of your mother's spell made you smell human to him."

"But now" Katrina sighed looking at Aria.

"Now you smell like Kiera and Katrina, wild, ancient, and strong." Gabriel finished.

"Your scent will attract the attention of any shifter." Xavier said.

"So, what, I can never be alone?" Aria asked, disbelief in every word.

"No." Gabriel said. "But we have become complacent. There hasn't been a strange wolf around in a long time. We didn't even think to be on alert, and one slipped right by us."

"I don't think we are complacent," Xavier said. "I've been thinking about this a lot." He looked at Gabriel out of respect to make sure he was alright with him continuing. At Gabriel's nod of approval, he continued. "At the pack meeting the night Aria was lost you passed around the branch with the strangers smell on it and only some of the pack could smell the stranger on it, some could not. We chalked it up to smelling ability, but Ryan was one of those who couldn't smell, and he is one of our best trackers by scent."

"But everyone else at Aria's smelled wolf?" Katrina questioned.

"But everyone else there had witch blood" Gabriel answered before Xavier could.

Xavier nodded. "Your mother had the gift, my mother had the gift, and obviously Brian and Chris's mother." he broke off gesturing towards Katrina. He continued as his arm fell to his side. "And I'm going to guess Cheri took in Natasha and Gage because Natasha had witch blood."

"Can I go?" Aria interrupted, acting as though she could care less about the conversation going on around her.

"You can go but Xavier will be going with you, and someone will relieve him around Midnight." Gabriel commanded. "Xavier, we can finish this conversation later."

Aria met Gage's eyes again. "Fine." She walked out of the room. Xavier grinned at Gabriel and followed her out.

"My truck is over here." Xavier pointed when Aria turned in the wrong direction.

"I said I needed space." Aria said not even turning to look at him.

Xavier sighed he had hoped she wouldn't be difficult. He was exhausted after fighting with the grizzly then chasing it and fighting with it again. "Aria, you have a choice, you can get in my truck, and I'll drive you home or I can stuff you in my truck and drive you home."

Aria slowed her pace but did not stop. Xavier was quickly losing his amusement. He started towards her to his surprise she whirled on him, "Who the hell do you think you are? Don't you dare give me ultimatums." She yelled at him.

"Look." He said, unclenching his balled fists and putting his hands up in a 'I surrender pose', "I know you are upset and in shock, but just like Gabriel said we cannot leave you alone. You can be in your house alone but not alone in the sense no one is looking out for you."

Aria wasn't sure what she wanted. Finally, she let go of some of the fear and said, "Can we run back to my house as wolves?"

Xavier would have been less shocked if she had sucker punched him. "If you want to?" He raised his eyebrows in question?

"Yes," Aria let out a long breath, "no," she sighed, "I don't know, I want to try it again, but I'm scared."

"Just get in the truck," Xavier began, reaching out for her, "and after you've had the night to ponder it Kiera, Gage, and I will come over tomorrow and we can try shifting some more. Does that sound like a plan?"

She stepped away from him, her moods changing lightning fast. "Fine, I'll let you know in the morning, but I'm walking home right now."

As she turned away from him, he started to argue some more then changed his mind. He reached out, spun her around, and threw her over his shoulder. "We're done discussing this." He growled, finally provoked by her attitude.

"Put me down." Aria demanded. She thought about kicking and hitting him but decided that would not be dignified. "I mean it Xavier."

"Alright" he said, opening his truck door and depositing her in the passenger side. "I put you down." He surveyed her angry red cheeks and the set of her mouth. "Save both of us from an exhausting battle and stay put. I have been training my whole life in combat. You won't win but you can tire me out and I'm positive you'd get in a good bite or two."

Aria sat there debating and finally crossed her arms over her chest and stared out the windshield completely ignoring him. Seeing she had decided to stay put he cautiously shut the door and hurried around the front of the truck, getting in the driver's side. "I'm sorry." He began as he started the truck and began to move forward. "Like Katrina said, we had no idea how to tell you." He risked a glance at her and saw she was sitting completely still with her arms crossed staring straight ahead. He decided to give her the time she had asked for and remain silent.

She jumped out of his truck the second he stopped when they got to her house a few minutes later. He put the truck in park and watched her go into the house. He knew she wanted to be alone, but she didn't understand the meaning of pack. The pack was more than family. Pack united together to protect each other, and she was in danger. They didn't all share familial blood, but they shared loyalty through their shifter identity and shared secrets. He hoped she would let herself experience the connection and unity of the pack when she calmed down. He saw from the corner of his eye Brian sitting under a tree at the edge of the woods in his wolf form ready to begin guard duty. As Xavier drove around the circle to exit the driveway, he rolled down his window to call out to Brian, "I'll be back around 2am to relieve you." Brian raised his muzzle in acknowledgement.

Chapter 7

Aria was so confused; she knew that her mom's family had just met her, and it made sense they would not know how to tell her she was a wolf. Especially since they had no idea what her mother had done to prevent her from changing. She had to admit at least to herself that she understood why they had not told her. She would have thought they were certifiably crazy. She was very grateful her father had only left that morning and had a run to Florida, he didn't know where he would be going after but she figured she had a couple weeks at least to get her head on straight before he returned and she had to act normal. She went up to her bedroom and grabbed the quilt her grandmother had made her out of her mother's clothes. She took it downstairs and lay down on the couch wrapping it around her. Her thoughts swirling around in her head. Tonight, the quilt gave her comfort because Grandma Ann had made it, not because it was made of her mother's things. She was angry at her mom, not just angry. She felt betrayed. Her thoughts continued to swirl around her mother, her father, Kiera, Katrina, Gabriel, Xavier, the pack, and the grizzly attack going around and around. She lay there for hours coming to no conclusion and finally fell into an uneasy sleep.

Aria was still sleeping when Xavier approached her house from the woods, Brian scented him before he saw him. Brian waited for Xavier's muzzle to nudge him before acknowledging him. In silent agreement they shifted back to humans. "How is she?" Xavier asked.

"She laid down on the couch and hasn't moved since you dropped her off. She was asleep last time I checked on her through the window." Brian scanned the woods. "I have a weird feeling something bad is going to happen."

Xavier inhaled long and slow scenting the night. "Something feels off, I agree, but I can't smell anything so it must not be here yet."

"Are you sure you should be here alone?" Brian asked. "I keep fearing someone or something has gotten past me, so I keep checking on her through the windows, so I don't wake her up."

Xavier inhaled again, taking in the breeze and evaluating his own gut. "My pride wants to say I'll be fine." He let out a huff, "but Gabriel keeps telling me to think through my pride and make better choices. I'll call Gabriel before you leave and ask for a second or third guard." As Brian was reaching for the backpack he had carried over. Xavier's phone began to ring. Xavier smiled at Brian, guessing who was calling.

"Dad." Brian said half amused, half worried.

"Hello" Xavier answered the phone. "Are you, Brian, and Aria alright?"

"Yes," Xavier answered promptly. "But Brian and I were just discussing how something feels off. I was just about to call you and request one or two additional guards."

"Well done," Gabriel praised. "I'm going to call Greg and have some of the deputies join you in case it is needed." Gabriel knew that when Xavier took over in a few years, having such a young Alpha had the potential to cause problems but so far, the pack supported Xavier being trained and tonight he felt proud Xavier exhibited good judgment.

Within an hour Brian had left, and 3 deputies were on watch in wolf form with Xavier. They had left their vehicles at Gabriel's so they wouldn't alert Aria or delay an attack if one were imminent. Xavier was incredibly grateful for whatever magic allowed them to shift with their clothing. Only natural fibers shifted so the pack was often picky about what type of fabrics they wore, 100% cotton was a big favorite. The pack had found a place online that sold modern looking clothes made with nothing synthetic. When on guard duty pack members would often bring a satchel, they could carry in their mouths. In the satchel they had cell phones and shoes, since rubber soles did not shift, but their natural fiber socks did. The deputies carried their badges, guns, utility belts, shoes, and car keys over to Aria's house.

Xavier, David, Danny, and Miles were all settled listening to the sounds of the night. A couple hours later they were listening to a barred owl, each amused at the owl's hoot that sounded like someone asking "who cooks for you," when they heard a vehicle approaching. Their ears perked, as discussed earlier, Miles quickly shifted to human to call Gabriel. Gabriel answered on the first ring, "we are on our way." Miles set the phone down having never spoken and shifted back.

With that Miles hung up and nodded at the others who spread out a bit along the tree line. The vehicle was a utility vehicle and had 3 wolves in human form in it. Including the stranger who had been there previously and who escaped Gabriel and Gage at the bed and breakfast. Katrina had looked through her mother's old books and found a spell to cloak the smell of those on guard duty. Therefore, when the three unwelcome strangers exited the car, they did not immediately smell the wolves in the tree line. Gabriel was already there and shifted as he approached Xavier. Brian, Chris, and Ryan were behind him, and they stayed in their wolf form.

"I don't smell wolf," said one of the men.

"I told you, the human lives here." Glen snapped. He was really fed up with his two traveling companions. They were only good for thug work, and he grew tired of their stupidity.

"So, what, are we going to get the human to tell us where the little she wolf you saw lives?" The other man questioned.

"Yes, Alpha will want her, she is special." Glen was about to walk up the stone path to the house when Gabriel stepped through the trees near the woodshed and made himself known.

"Good morning, Can I help you?" Gabriel's voice was low and dangerous.

Glen was completely surprised, how had he not smelled the human? "Good morning, sir." Glen began. He had no idea what to say and decided things had just gotten a lot messier with the girl's father here. "We were looking for a house that was listed for sale."

"Really, at 4 a.m.?" Gabriel raised his dark eyebrows in question.

The other two looked at Glen wondering why he was bothering to make conversation with this insignificant human. "Just get rid of him" one of the thugs said.

Glen held up a hand in a wait motion he thought something was off. "Well sir, you are up early. We just got into town, and we were so excited. We thought we'd drive up and get a look at the property."

"This place is not for sale." Gabriel rubbed his chin as if he were trying to think hard. "As a matter of fact, I do not believe there is a place for sale within 20 miles of here."

Glen was sure something was off now, but he couldn't think of how to subtly tell the thugs with him.

Just then one of the thugs made a mistake, "We need to talk to your girl and then we'll leave. If you cooperate no one will get hurt." the thug threatened.

Glen growled, "What the hell are you doing?"

"You're wasting our time with small talk." The thug snapped at Glen.

Gabriel smiled, it penetrated through the thug's arrogance, he felt fear wash over him. "I have no intention of cooperating. However, I'm afraid you are very wrong about no one getting hurt."

Gabriel lifted his arms straight out to his sides encompassing the yard as 4 wolves and two huge brown bears walked slowly into the yard. "Why do you want to talk to the girl who lives here?"

"Why couldn't we smell you? Why are there bear shifters with your pack?" Glen asked, taking an instinctive step back as his wolf told him to retreat to live.

"Maybe you should research the pack you are dealing with before you trespass." Gabriel advised. "I will not ask again, why do you want to talk to the girl who lives here?"

"We wanted to find out about your pack, we saw her with one of your pack and thought it would be safer to ask a human who knows about you rather than the pack itself." Glen lied.

"He's lying." Katrina told Gabriel as she stepped out of the trees.

Gabriel nodded and his pack started to close in. Before anyone but Katrina registered the move the thugs pulled out tranquilizer guns and started to fire. Katrina's shield spell was faster than the darts but only because she had sensed the movement.

"Protectie." The darts fell at the shield. Glen and the thugs were so shocked they almost missed the opportunity to get in the vehicle and get out of there.

The pack raced forward to catch them, but it was too late, the three trespassers were in the vehicle and pulling away.

"Dammit," Gabriel exclaimed. "Xavier, Ryan, Miles, and Danny stay here." He shifted as he ran towards the wood line to his house. Katrina and the rest of the pack followed. When they arrived at Gabriel's and Katrina's house they got in their vehicles and went to see if they could catch the trespassers. There were more pack members at the house now. Everyone had received a text message. Thanks to modern technology a group text with all members meant everyone received a warning at once. The sheriff had sent out an APB on the vehicle tagged as needing to be questioned for information about a robbery attempt. Gabriel hoped they would locate the three men by daybreak.

Aria woke suddenly startled by the sound of the fray going on in her yard. She ran to the front door in time to see the vehicle race out of her yard. She watched Gabriel, Katrina, and a bunch of the pack run towards Kiera's house. She saw a brown bear and 3 wolves. Xavier sensed her and turned towards her.

"What happened?" she asked as she ran out the front door, forgetting for the moment she was mad at all of them.

Xavier paused to make sure he still heard the vehicle fading into the distance before he shifted back to human. "There were strange men here looking for you." Xavier explained, walking towards her. "But it sounds like they were looking for you because of the pack."

"Until tonight I didn't even know there was a pack?" Aria pointed out.

Xavier thought that through, "What were you doing the day you got lost in the woods the first few days you were here?"

"Kiera and I went to school, after school we went shopping and got some ice cream." She remembered that day well, it was the first day she had really connected with her cousin.

"Dammit they were looking for Kiera." Xavier ran to the edge of the yard to grab his satchel. He pulled out his cell phone and dialed. "Gabriel, they were looking for Kiera."

Aria could not make out specific words, but she could hear Gabriel's voice rise in exclamation. "Yes, I'll call them now," Xavier said. "Gabriel, Gage would die before he would let anyone hurt Kiera." With that he hung up the phone and looked at Aria. "I know you are in an information overload, but I need you to pack a bag and come back home with me."

"Why?" Aria asked.

"There are at least three strange wolves and until we can confirm there are not more, we need to make sure everyone is safe." Xavier explained, hoping she would not put up a fight.

"They were after Kiera?" Aria asked.

Xavier nodded, "Yes, and they seem to think you are the key to finding her. We are stronger together. If we are all in the same place, we will be able to protect each other better."

Aria deliberated quickly, "Alright give me 10-15 minutes." With that she turned back into the house, no matter how angry she was, she would not take people away from protecting Kiera.

Xavier sighed in relief and texted Gabriel with an update. "Miles, can you please go get my truck, so she doesn't have to carry her stuff through the woods? Her car is still at the park. The keys are on top of the visor." Miles, still in wolf form nodded and disappeared into the trees.

Aria had just come out when Miles appeared with the truck. Xavier looked at her in black sweatpants with a black hoodie that had Philadelphia printed in white capital letters across the front. She had on dark crocs and a duffel bag slung over her shoulder. Her golden red hair was pulled back into a braid. He went up to her and took the duffel. "Let me carry that."

Miles jumped out of the truck and handed Xavier the keys. "I'll grab my bag, and we can go." Xavier opened the passenger side and slid the duffel in the middle, he stepped back and let Aria climb in. Once she was in, he shut the door. He went to the back of the truck and took the satchels from the wolves and set them in the bed, the wolves, including Miles who had shifted back to his wolf form, leapt gracefully into the bed of the truck. Xavier closed the tailgate and went to get into the driver's seat. When they arrived at Kiera's, Aria was exhausted and had so many questions she didn't know where to start.

Xavier guessed what she was thinking. "It can all wait till morning." He said dropping the tailgate for the wolves.

"It is morning." Aria pointed out.

Xavier looked towards the moon, "yes, but none of us has slept much so what I should have said is after we all get some rest."

Aria rolled her eyes, "Fine, where do I sleep?"

"With me" Kiera chimed in. Aria hadn't noticed when she'd come outside.

Aria smiled, "Lead the way trouble."

Kiera laughed, "Very funny Dora."

Xavier felt a knot loosen in his shoulders; it would be a lot easier to defend everyone in one place. He turned to get some rest greeting those who were staying up on guard duty as he passed them. He hoped Gabriel and the others caught up with the three trespassers.

Later that day when the sky was brilliant blue, and the sun shone over the mountains the pack gathered. Aria was staring around at everyone; she had no idea how large the pack was. She even recognized her English and Gym teachers, not to mention the principal.

Chapter 8

Kiera had spent the morning explaining the pack hierarchy and all of the intricacies of pack culture. She even explained to Aria how Xavier would be Alpha one day. Kiera thought it was a bit funny that Xavier was being taught by wolves he would lead in just a few years. For the most part they were a peaceful pack who lived their lives like a close-knit community. The Alpha rarely had to enforce specific rules because the pack mostly lived in harmony. Kiera confided in Aria that she thought her dad would have to become stricter about rules. Aria thought of Gabriel who was tall with dark gypsy like features. His eyes were obsidian and his hair the color of raven feathers. He was a contrast to Xavier. Whose eyes were Caribbean blue with pale hair topping his head.

Aria walked around the tables of food and noticed there was a lot of fruit salad, sweets, and smoked fish. She had to wonder if the bear in the male pack members showed a preference for food a bear would eat. Gabriel grilled beef and Elk steaks, bison burgers, and chicken. These food choices made her wonder if the wolves inside of them preferred meat. She couldn't tell if Gabriel was an exceptional cook or if after her wolf was unbound her food preferences changed because the food smelled delicious.

The weather had been unseasonably warm so the pack meeting was held outside on the lawn, turning to brown as the temperatures dropped below freezing at night. Gabriel stood up and the crowd sitting on the lawn silenced immediately. "As most of you know Aria shifted yesterday." He paused "and we had trouble yesterday." Gabriel explained what happened at Aria's as well as the previous time the stranger had been in town.

After several pack members asked questions, Gabriel laid out the plans he had to protect everyone. "The deputies will take turns on the 3 access points into the area. Outsiders will think they are looking for speeders or possibly people running drugs to and from Canada. Aria will stay with us when her father is on the road until we are certain she is safe at her house. I don't want any young wolves going out alone." He scanned the crowd, "actually I don't want any wolves alone. If you go out, go out in pairs. If you live alone, we will set up a check in system. Katrina will let you know who your check in person is. I want a check in every time you come and go from your house as well as an evening and morning check in."

After the guard and check in schedules were created, they had food. Besides what the pack had grilled, everyone had brought something to contribute. The pack treated the meal like a welcome party for Aria, welcoming her to the pack. After stuffing herself she lay on the grass feeling the slight breeze bring out goosebumps over her skin. She felt the wind and the grass like she had never felt them before. She wondered if shifting for the first time had awakened senses in her that had been suppressed by whatever spell her mother had performed on her. Kiera was sitting with Gage and Xavier, she nudged them and nodded towards Aria. They all looked at her laying with her jeans and the same black Philadelphia sweatshirt she had been wearing earlier, her feet back in the dark crocs. They could all smell the chill in the air and figured snow would come soon. They had already had the ice storm. They all walked over to Aria, Kiera and Xavier laid down on either side of Aria Gage laid down on the other side of Kiera. Xavier took Aria's hand as Kiera took Aria's other hand and Gage's hand. The four of them lay there linked.

"How are you doing?" Kiera squeezed Aria's hand.

"I'm alright." Aria sighed.

"Do you forgive us?" Kiera couldn't help but ask."

"I do, I get how hard it must have been for you all to decide how to tell me. I'm still hurt and mad at my mom, but a lot of good that does me." Aria sighed again, it would do no good to be angry at her dead mother. She finally expressed her real worry. "What am I going to tell my father?"

"Nothing," Gage sat up and looked over Kiera at Aria. "He may have a harder time accepting it with your anger and doubt still so fresh. I suggest just not changing while he's home and once you get everything straight with yourself speak with Gabriel and Katrina and go from there."

Xavier and Kiera were watching Aria's face as Gage spoke and saw her brows relax. "You're right." Aria agreed, "He won't be home for a while, I'll take it one step at a time." Kiera squeezed Gage's hand in thanks. Xavier shot him a grateful look.

Kiera sat up and grinned at Aria. "Want to go run?"

Aria frowned at her in question, "I have never been much of a runner?"

Kiera giggled and the guys grinned, "I don't mean a jog, I mean a run, a real run as wolves." Kiera looked towards the expansive gray mountains tipped with pure white jetting out browning forest and Aria swore her eyes glowed, "You've never experienced anything like a run up a mountain as a wolf."

"Can you?" Aria questioned Kiera, "Don't your ribs hurt?"

"They are a bit sore but the more I shift the faster I'll heal. So long as I don't overdo it and eat a lot, I'll be fine!" Kiera explained.

Aria saw Xavier and Gage follow Kiera's gaze and felt their excitement. "Go!" Katrina had overheard them talking. "Show her how it feels to be a wolf. Just be careful, stay on the preserve."

"We will." Gage assured her.

"There is no car access, and those city wolves are not going to be going for a run in our wilderness." Xavier elaborated.

Aria bid goodbye to the pack that had so graciously welcomed her and went with her friends.

Aria was terrified to shift and didn't really know how. Gabriel helped her by talking her through the process. Once she was a wolf, he counseled her to stretch, to take deep breaths, to center herself, and to listen to her wolf. Once her shift was complete, she felt the wolf begin to merge with herself and the fear began to fade. She recognized her wolf as the part of her that was brave and fierce. She whined at Gabriel in thanks and turned to follow the others. Aria couldn't stop looking at Xavier in wolf form. He was otherworldly with his Caribbean blue eyes and silver coat. She shook herself and followed the others to the edge of the yard.

They started out slowly. Aria was amazed at the amount of life the forest held. Her senses picked up smells, sounds, and an otherness her human senses had never noticed. She knew now why her mother had loved to camp so much. She remembered the overnight hiking trips she had taken with her mom. Her mom had always been comfortable in the wild. She realized her mom's love and comfort with the wild had grown her love for it as well. Changing into a wolf had made her more comfortable with it. It was easier to relax in the vast wilderness when you were an apex predator at the top of the food chain. Even through her anger she felt for the first time in a long time that she was connected to her mother.

Kiera gave Aria the first mile to think, to acclimate, and then she picked up the pace. Gage and Xavier matched her speed, Aria increased hers as well. By the time they hit the fifth mile Aria had processed her feelings and felt pure joy as she ran.

They ran past rabbits, elk, mule deer, mountain sheep, and even a moose. Aria's senses picked out each unique smell. She was in love with the run. Even as the temperature dropped as they climbed further up the mountain, she was comfortable. Aria was amazed at how much stamina she had. She was only a little tiring as they climbed. Soon there was white snow beneath their paws and the air was crisp. Finally, they must have reached the spot that Kiera had in mind because the other three slowed and trotted around a large gray rock. Gage who was in the front lay down, Kiera laid down next to him. Xavier stood waiting for Aria as she walked around the rock. She almost stopped breathing. The sight before her was so breathtakingly beautiful. They were high up and it seemed as though they could see forever. Majestic peaks and rolling valleys stretched out endlessly before them. As big as they were, the expansive blue sky was so expansive it dwarfed the mountains. Xavier nudged her over towards Kiera where she lay down next to her cousin, Xavier laying down next to her. She just kept staring at the sight. Several eagles were soaring almost too high to believe. She could hear a hawk's hunting cry and see the darkening sky to the east. The four lay there in comfortable silence taking in the world before them while the whole sky turned deep blue, the thin line of orange disappearing in the distance. Aria jumped up looking around in panic as she realized how dark it was.

The others tensed, using their senses to search for the danger that had startled Aria. They looked around and realized she must be concerned about the fading light. Xavier shifted to human. "Are you worried about the dark?" He asked. She nodded at him realizing she probably didn't look like a real wolf bobbing her head up and down. "Don't worry you have good night vision, as well as an amazing sense of smell, and on top of that you have a sixth sense about your surroundings that is ingrained in you." Xavier reached out and scratched her ear, "Would you feel better if I ran back as a bear? No animal on these mountains will mess with a group containing brown bears and wolves."

Aria thought about it and nodded. She was still worried about her own encounter with the grizzly. "Alright Gage and I will shift to brown bears and follow you and Kiera down the mountain." Kiera came up alongside Aria nuzzling her while Xavier and Gage shifted to their bear form. The run back down the darkening mountain into the black depths of the valley was exhilarating. The night animals quieted as two brown bears running with two wolves streaked through the quiet night. Even a mountain lion slunk further away from the path, deciding the group was too much of a threat. They caught the smell of the cat, noted it and kept moving. The smell and sound of predators alerted every rabbit and every mouse. Only an owl hooted in the night unconcerned about the earth bound predators. They caught the distant smell of a real bear, but it was distant enough they were not likely to run into the animal. The pack was always aware of the location of the real wolf pack that lived nearby and knew they were on the other side of the valley. As they ran Xavier thought he would have to go over some safety concerns with Aria about the local wildlife. Even though they were apex predators a wolf could be injured if it was careless.

They made it back to the house. Aria figured she would stay with Kiera again tonight but knew she would have to discuss with Gabriel and Katrina what precautions they would need to take for her to be able to stay at her own house again. She was certain her dad would freak out if he thought they were in danger.

They shifted back to humans in Kiera's yard and bid each other goodnight. Aria thanked Gage and Xavier and followed Kiera inside. Aria and Kiera told Katrina about the run as they drank the rose hip tea she had made them. Katrina was hopeful Aria was starting to accept her identity. They got ready for bed and, exhausted from the last two days, they fell asleep as soon as their heads hit their pillows.

Chapter 9

Aria woke up and realized she would have to go to school. She wasn't sure how she would handle Kelsey. She got up dressed in jeans and a sweatshirt, noting the frost on the window and decided to add a thermal shirt under her sweatshirt. Kiera came in already dressed in a high waisted plaid skirt with thick wool tights and a cropped sweater. Aria looked up at her "How do you always find those super cute outfits?"

Kiera looked down at her purple sweater, purple and black plaid skirt, and thick black wool tights. "I shop online."

Aria looked down at her jeans and hoodie, "Your outfits are as cute as Hannah's on one of the YouTube channels I watch. I need to know which sites you're on!"

The girls rode to the school with Xavier and Gage. Normally everyone left at different times and did their own thing, but this morning Brian and the others followed them in. Gabriel and Katrina insisted on a text when they made it safely to the school. Xavier gave Aria's hand an encouraging squeeze when she looked at the school with trepidation. "She's nothing, ignore her." Xavier leaned into Aria, "nothing" he breathed in her ear. Shivers ran through her body at his closeness and his warm breath caressing her ear.

Aria nodded and walked towards the school. Aria made it to her locker before she caught a glimpse of Kelsey standing with the other senior girls who followed her around. She could feel Kelsey's eyes on her and just knew Kelsey was going to approach her. She thought of what Kiera would do, fierce, brave little Kiera would probably turn around, walk up to Kelsey, and get the confrontation over with. Aria loved Kiera's character but that wasn't her. She decided to patiently wait until Kelsey approached her. Aria wasn't scared of Kelsey, she just decided not to borrow trouble. Kelsey didn't bother to wait long. "You look fine to me." Kelsey sneered as she approached Aria's locker.

"Excuse me?" Aria asked, turning around.

"Everyone was freaking out about poor little you all alone in the big bad woods." Kelsey's voice was high and condescending. "Like a little red riding hood, all alone in the big bad woods."

Aria just looked at her as if waiting for her to make a point. "I'm not sure what you want me to say Kelsey." Aria almost started to laugh as she imagined what Kelsey would say if she knew what really happened in the woods.

Kelsey was taken a bit off guard by Aria's cool calm. "You have everyone thinking you are a sweet little innocent city girl come to the big bad woods of Montana. The cops said a bear almost hurt you and now the park is closed till next year."

"Kelsey, what happened in the woods is none of your business." Aria kept direct eye contact with her. "I took your dare as a good sport since we were playing a game. I didn't realize the risks and I shouldn't have assumed you were a decent human being who wouldn't give someone a dangerous dare." Aria held up her hand when it appeared that Kelsey was going to interrupt. "I'm not finished. I have no idea what your problem with me is as I barely know you, but I find I don't care. If you don't like me that's fine, then stay away from me and we don't have to be around each other." Aria turned and walked away, noting Xavier by the corner. He held out his hand and she decided to walk to him. Neither Xavier nor Aria saw the blind rage, caused by jealousy, bloom over Kelsey's face as they walked away.

"How was school?" Katrina asked the girls as they walked into the kitchen to get an after school snack.

Kiera smiled. "Aria told Kelsey off yesterday. So, all day yesterday and today Kelsey keeps trying to make jokes about Little Red Riding Hood to get under Aria's skin."

Katrina looked at Aria in question. "She says I'm a pathetic helpless city girl, who is acting like a victim and since she's heard I was attacked by a wild animal she is trying to make it an insult." Aria explained.

"But we think it is hilarious!" Kiera giggled.

"Also, Little Red Riding Hood took an ax to the wolf, so I guess she wasn't so helpless after all." Gabriel added as he walked out of the kitchen.

Katrina, Kiera, and Aria all started laughing. They all heard a vehicle pull up outside. "Greg is here." Gabriel announced from the front of the house.

"Greg is the Sheriff of our county." Kiera explained to Aria. "He is also part of the pack. He is on the council and a member of the guard. He was out of town when we had your welcome picnic."

Gabriel headed to the front of the house to let Greg in. Katrina, Kiera, and Aria kept talking about school that day ignoring the murmured voices coming from the front door.

Gabriel and Greg walked back into where they were sitting. Gabriel looked at Katrina and she knew immediately something was very wrong. "What?" Is all she asked her husband.

"Aria this is Greg, he is the Sheriff. He just got back into town last night." Gabriel introduced Greg not knowing Kiera had already told her who he was. "He needs to talk to you. I think it's best if you sit down."

"You're scaring me," Aria told Gabriel, collapsing into a chair. "What is it? Tell me."

Greg walked over to Aria and pulled a chair over in front of her. He sat down and placed his hands on her knees to comfort her. "Aria there's no easy way to say this. I received a call from a Sergeant Colby from West Memphis, Arkansas."

"What's wrong with my dad?" Aria asked, her heart dropped into her stomach as her legs started to tingle in a numbing fear. She knew it was her dad, he was supposed to have left Arkansas early this morning.

"Your dad was killed at the West Memphis truck stop last night." Greg moved his hands to grasp hers as he spoke the words, he knew would change her life forever.

Aria's face went pale, her large hazel eyes glistened with tears that had not yet fallen. Katrina walked over to hold her. "Why does everyone I love die?!" she screamed the question as the tears began to gush down her cheeks.

Kiera joined her mother, and they wrapped their arms around Aria in an emotion filled embrace, to keep her together through her grief and to give her a safe space to fall apart. They pushed all their feelings of love and caring into her, hoping she would feel them and know that she wasn't alone. She was loved and she would be taken care of. Aria couldn't stop crying. "What happened?" She managed to sob out.

"The sergeant said he was killed in the parking lot of the truck stop walking back to his truck." Greg put his hands back on her knees wanting to comfort her as well. One of the worst parts of his job was informing family members they had lost a loved one. It was a rare thing thankfully. He remembered having to tell Katrina when her own parents had died. "Aria, there's going to be an investigation and an autopsy so if they catch the person that did this, they can convict them."

"How did he die?" Aria asked, clarifying what she wanted to know as Gabriel knelt on her other side to help console her.

Greg looked to Katrina and Gabriel to see if he should answer her question. "He was stabbed," Greg responded when he received a nod from Katrina.

"She will do better knowing." Katrina told Greg holding Aria tighter as she broke into uncontrollable sobs at the words.

Xavier had come into the room and heard. Gabriel signaled him to come over and take his place by Aria. "Katrina book me, Xavier, Danny, Ryan, and Brian a flight to Memphis as soon as you can." Gabriel told her as he rose.

All of them looked up at Gabriel. "You don't think this was random?" Xavier asked.

"No, and I know you want to stay here with Aria, but this will be a good learning experience for you. We have to move fast before the scent is gone, it may already be too late if it's rained over the last few days." Gabriel said. "There will be enough protection here and we'll be quick."

Katrina kissed Aria and squeezed her hands. "I'll go book it now."

"I'll call Danny and Ryan to tell them to meet you at the airport." Greg rose, pulling his cell phone out of his pocket.

Gabriel knelt in front of Aria as Katrina went into her home office to book them a flight out of the city, "I'm so sorry." Gabriel clasped her hands, "I'm so very sorry, it didn't even occur to me they would target Joel, and it should have. I cannot tell you how sorry I am." Gabriel felt miserable, how could he not have realized the only vulnerable pack member was Joel. He was pack even though he didn't know it and he was alone driving around the United States.

"They did their research." Xavier realized.

"Yes, and they're letting us know they're not done with us." Gabriel confirmed.

"How do you know?" Aria asked.

"That's why he's going to Memphis," Kiera pointed to her dad, "to confirm it was the thug wolves we saw." Kiera guessed.

Gabriel nodded, "Yes we need to confirm."

"After you confirm we will need to prepare for them to come at us again." Greg warned his alpha.

"We will." Gabriel assured Greg. "When I get back, I would like your thoughts on that."

"I'll put some ideas together." Greg had lots of ideas on how to help defend their territory and keep their secret.

Gabriel looked into Aria's eyes. Her huge hazel eyes were red, and tears were still flowing down her cheeks. "You are not alone; we will always take care of you."

Aria met his eyes, "I don't blame you. I never thought of Dad either." She took a deep breath in. "I want to stay in our home, but I don't know how I'm going to support myself."

Gabriel looked puzzled. "Honey, I'm sure your dad had a life insurance policy but even if he didn't your grandparents left you a sizable trust fund."

Aria looked shocked, "Dad never said anything about that."

"He wanted you to have it when you turned 18 and were ready to start out on your own." Katrina told Aria walking back into the room. "He said he wanted to support you as long as he could so you could have all of the money when you turned 18." She turned to Gabriel, "You have to leave in 30 minutes to make it to the airport in time."

Gabriel nodded and looked at Xavier. "Let's go."

Once everyone had left Aria sat with tears still running down her cheeks. She was staring at nothing and felt a hole start to form in her chest. Katrina and Kiera helped Aria to the couch. Kiera lay next to her and held her cousin. She lay, holding her cousin until Aria cried herself to sleep.

"Do you think that she will be alright?" Kiera asked her mother.

"It's a corny phrase, but only time really will heal her." Katrina reassured her daughter. "It will be a long road, but she is strong, and she has us. We will help her."

Gabriel, Xavier, Danny, Ryan, and Brian were back in two days. They confirmed the wolves that were at Aria's house were the same ones that killed Joel. Aria mostly felt numb, but it was punctuated with overwhelming grief that seemed to consume her. Katrina, Kiera, Gage, and Xavier spent a lot of time with her. She stayed home from school until she felt she could make it through an entire day without dissolving into tears when it hit her, her dad was truly gone.

Chapter 10

It took a while for the authorities in Arkansas to release Joel's body. Gabriel and Katrina helped Aria start the emancipation process. Greg was able to reassure the county circuit court judge Aria's aunt and uncle were taking care of her until the emancipation paperwork was finalized. The pack members would take turns dropping off food and of course took turns checking on her. She had to arrange her finances so that she had an account to pay the bills and life's expenses. Perhaps the hardest part of becoming an adult was having to plan her dad's funeral. She had decided to bury him next to her mother here in Montana. Her father had sent her mother to Montana for burial at the request of her family, it was one of the things that made it easier to leave upstate New York. She had her memories of her mother in her heart and since she had been laid to rest elsewhere it had no longer felt like home without her.

Aria buried her father on a cold November day. The sky seemed to mourn with her as she drove home from the funeral reception. The sky was spitting out a mix of sleet and snow as if it too was crying. She knew she was being followed by someone from the pack. When she unlocked her house and went inside, she knew whoever it was would lay in the woods line and watch over her. She had stayed at Katrina's for a bit until Gabriel had set up motion activated cameras around the perimeter of her house far enough out, they could get to Aria before whatever intruder, or intruders had tripped the alarm. She was used to being in the house alone since Joel had been gone so much. Alone, she was back to that word. She felt that she was so alone it hurt. Her mother had been so loving and wonderful, but Aria realized she had never really known her mother. Her grandmother had been fun and full of life, but Aria's time with her had been so brief in the end. And as for her dad, well she couldn't believe her rock was gone. She had loved her father, and he had been there for her through all of her losses. He had comforted her, loved her, supported her, and now he was gone. She had never felt so alone in her whole life. She made sure all the doors were locked and went upstairs. She decided she needed a shower, hoping it would wash away the grief. When Aria got into the shower, the numbness dissolved instead of the grief, as though the water was washing it from her. She lost the remaining strength that had held her together through the last couple of weeks and sank to the floor, beginning to sob. The loneliness crashed over her; she began to drown in it. Her grief was so complete she didn't notice the passing of time or even the warm soothing water turning bitter cold. She was so consumed by grief and loneliness she stayed in a ball on the floor of the shower, the now frigid water running over her unnoticed. She didn't move when the bathroom door opened. She hardly noticed, not caring if it was an enemy coming to take her or kill her, just at that moment she felt that the loneliness was going to swallow her whole anyway.

Xavier's heart broke when he saw her. She didn't even seem to notice he had come in. When Brian called, worried about how long Aria had been in the bathroom, Xavier had come right over. After another 15 minutes of waiting to see if she came out, he used the emergency key he had and went in to check on her. When he reached in to shut the water off it was frigid. The pure cold water ignited his temper. He breathed in slow and steady to control the rising anger. He grabbed a towel from the counter and wrapped her in it. He was not looking at her nakedness, he only saw her pale broken face streaked with red. Her hazel eyes outlined in crimson from crying. He picked her up and set her on her bed. He went to her drawers and found a pair of pajama pants and shirt. He dressed her as though she was a child purposely looking at her wrecked face as to not violate her privacy. After she was dressed, he used a towel to dry her hair. She sat with tears leaking out of her eyes staring at nothing. He brushed her hair and braided it. Then he wrapped her in the quilt she had at the end of the bed and held her close. He sang an old folk song he remembered from his grandmother in her native tongue. Her tears stopped and her eyelids began to close. She finally fell asleep from sheer exhaustion. Xavier texted Katrina to let her know he was staying with Aria and held her all night dozing on and off.

Aria woke up feeling safe and warm. Xavier sensed her wake up. He gave her a moment to orient herself. Aria snuggled into the safety and warmth and began to drift back to sleep when reality came rushing to her. She sat bolt upright, nearly hitting Xavier in the chin. "What happened?" Aria looked down at herself, "How, where, what?" She was lost. "I remember getting into the shower in a daze and then I don't remember anything else. How did you get here?" Aria questioned.

Xavier sat up straighter and looked her in the eyes, "Brian called when you didn't come out of the bathroom. He saw the light go on in the window, but it never turned off." Xavier paused to give her time to remember, when she nodded, he continued, "We got worried. Katrina and Kiera were still in town cleaning up the reception hall. I let myself in and checked on you. You were sitting in freezing cold water crying and shaking. I wrapped you in a towel, put some pajamas on you, wrapped you in your quilt, and sat with you all night." He went silent again, letting her process.

"Did I have clothes on in the shower?" Aria asked, looking down, her face turning bright red. No one had ever seen her naked, well except her parents when she was a baby.

"No," Xavier looked down as well to save her some more embarrassment. "Aria, I averted my eyes and dressed you without looking. I respected your privacy as best I could. Please don't be embarrassed." He hoped she believed him.

Aria looked at him and felt herself relax slightly when she saw no leer, no knowing glance at her body. His honesty and sincerity put her at ease. She thought she may be embarrassed when she thought about it again later but decided not to dwell on it now.

"Do you want to hurt yourself?" Xavier asked her.

"What?" Aria was surprised by the question, "Why would you ask that?"

"Aria, when I got here you were purple and blue and shaking from the cold water. You didn't even seem to notice when I walked in the bathroom." Xavier exclaimed, working hard to keep the anger he felt at the state he found her in out of his voice.

"No, I," She let out a sigh, "I had just been bottling up all of my emotions and the loneliness overwhelmed me."

Xavier believed her but also thought she should not be alone for long stretches of time until she had been given more time to process the grief. "Can I use your downstairs bathroom?" Xavier asked.

"Yes, of course," Aria replied. "I'll get dressed and meet you downstairs."

"I'll make you some tea and breakfast." Xavier told her as he stood up and left her room.

"I'm not hungry." She told his back.

"I didn't ask you if you were hungry" Xavier pointed out as he walked out of the bedroom.

Aria brushed her teeth, washed her face, and braided her hair. She pulled on black yoga pants and a black t-shirt with lavender flowers all over it. She looked at herself in the mirror. Who was the strange girl looking back at her? Her face was gaunt. She had dark purple under her red puffy eyes. She looked like she had been through hell and back. She supposed she had been. She wasn't sure what came next. When the initial wave of grief had hit her, it was all consuming. Her grief had come in waves, but she always had a purpose. She had to file for emancipation, then she had to get set up living on her own, then she had to plan her father's funeral. Now she just had to live, she thought that might be the hardest part yet. She pulled on some socks before going downstairs to see what Xavier had made her for breakfast. She had to remind herself not to think about Xavier seeing her naked as she started down the stairs.

Aria was pleasantly surprised to see a cup of tea and two pieces of toast. "Thank you." She looked up at Xavier. She wanted him to see she was very sincere in her gratitude; he was not trying to stuff her full of eggs and bacon. Toast and peppermint tea were exactly right, and it made her feel like she may actually be able to accomplish living through this. Xavier smiled sitting down next to her enjoying a companionable silence as they ate.

"Are you up for coming to Thanksgiving?" Katrina asked Aria later that day.

"Yes," Aria said, "Can I bring something?"

"You don't have to bring anything." Katrina told her.

"I'd like to bring something." Aria smiled, "I used to make Thanksgiving dinner with my mom, then with my grandma Ann, I like cooking."

"Alright" Katrina thought about it. "You can make pumpkin pies, or green bean casserole, and or another dessert. We make a lot of everything since the whole pack or most of us all celebrate together."

Aria thought about it, "If you send someone over to help me bring it here, I'll make 4 pumpkin pies, 2 green bean casseroles, and 2 pans of chocolate lasagna."

Katrina reached over and hugged Aria smiling, "That sounds like a plan!"

Aria was laying on her couch watching her favorite YouTube channel, Hannah Lee Duggan, and thinking about the day. She had spent the whole morning cooking, then Kiera and Xavier had come over to help her bring the food over to Katrina's house to celebrate Thanksgiving in the afternoon. The whole pack and their families came, everyone bringing food. All of the pack members' families were shifters with the exception of some spouses. Gabriel, Chris, Brian, and Gage had set up tables all over the house in the living room, dining room, family room, and kitchen. They had even set up tables in the attached garage making sure there was room for everyone. While Katrina and Kiera had made traditional thanksgiving food like turkey, mashed potatoes, and stuffing, other pack members brought traditional food from all over to celebrate and give thanks for the pack. Greg's wife had brought Cabbage rolls and sweet bread made in traditional Romanian fashion. Mr. Carr the high school principal and his family brought traditional Irish stew. Aria thought she had been able to try food from all over western and eastern Europe. She had enjoyed the day. As she lay there reflecting on the day she felt the loss of her dad again. She let the tears come but they didn't consume her this time.

She got into a routine over the coming weeks. It snowed a lot before Christmas which was both joyful and sad. The pack began to relax a bit with no more signs of the intruders, but they did not become lazy. They kept working on strategies to keep everyone safe. There had been no signs of the strange wolves who had wanted to take Kiera so badly they were willing to kill Aria's father to make the pack suffer. They continued trying to track down the origin of the men who had killed Joel, but they didn't have much luck. Aria often thought about these faceless men who had taken her father from her but felt safe with the motion activated cameras Gabriel had set up. Twice the cameras had alerted, causing Gabriel, Xavier, and Gage to jump out of bed only to see a moose on the video feed. It had crossed Gabriel's mind that the strangers may attempt to use other shifters to gain access, and although it was rare to find shifters who were not wolves, it was not unheard of.

They pack had read journals and heard stories that had been passed down throughout the generations about other shapeshifters. Silver Creek pack rarely met other shifters besides those of the pack that had the ability to shift into the brown bear. Katrina and Gabriel had met a fox shifter in Idaho once when they were visiting their friends from another pack. Cheri had told Katrina stories about moose, coyote, deer, and even eagle shifters but they were rare. Most of the time the only reason shifters knew they were meeting another shifter was by scent. Scent could be a tricky indicator, for example, if someone had a pet, they often had their pet's scent on them. It was easier to tell with shifters if the animal scent coming off the person was an exotic animal smell. It was unlikely a person would have an eagle for a pet. Shifters had to be very careful in today's modern society with cameras everywhere. This meant many of them lived in remote areas and kept to themselves.

Katrina decided to start looking for a warning spell that allowed a second alert if the intruder was not an actual animal. Katrina scanned through some of Cheri's older texts and found a spell that allowed a warning if a shifter crossed a threshold. They had to take possession of their property with a ritual Katrina found, then they were able to set up the threshold alarm. The ownership ritual required Katrina, Gabriel, Brian, Chris, Kiera, Xavier, and Gage to give a few drops of blood to take ownership of the land they lived on. Aria was required to give up a few drops of blood to take possession of her land as well. With the spells in place everyone felt more at ease. Aria was amused at the combination of modern technology and old-world magic that allowed her to stay in her home. Xavier, Kiera, and Gage visited her a lot, and once in a while she had other friends over. She was determined to show Katrina and Gabriel she could be responsible. She got up every morning, got ready for school, cooked her own meals, did her own laundry, took out the trash, paid her bills, and she bought groceries. She realized she had already done most of the day-to-day life things adults do because her father was away so much.

It was late January when she was on her way to school alone. Kiera stayed home in bed feeling a bit sick. Aria didn't realize the roads were slippery until she tried to stop for an elk and ended up in the ditch, like she had in the fall. She had just climbed out of her car and began to survey the situation when Xavier pulled up in his truck, Gage in the passenger seat. He rolled down his window, "I think you need bumpers along the driveway like in bowling." Xavier tried to say it with a straight face, but Gage didn't bother smothering his laugh.

"Very funny" Aria retorted dryly. "It's those stupid Elk, they are always making me slide off the road."

"Grab your backpack and get in, I'll call Gabriel."

When they got to school Gage rushed off to meet a teacher before class. Before Aria could turn and walk to her first class Xavier stopped her. "I was wondering if you would go to dinner with me on Valentine's Day?"

Aria went still "You mean kind of like a date?" she asked, feeling stupid but wanting to clarify.

"No, I mean exactly like a date." Xavier grinned at her.

She worked hard to prevent the blush she knew was creeping up her cheeks. "Well, I'll have to check my schedule." she said slyly.

"Your schedule huh?" Xavier looked a little exasperated. They had already been spending a lot of time together.

"Well, I read somewhere you shouldn't seem too eager to say yes when asked on a date." Aria smiled and headed towards her first class. "I'll let you know by the end of the day."

The day passed slowly as Aria thought about Xavier's date proposal. When the final bell rang, she hurried to get out of the school. She made sure to relax her pace once she stepped outside and started towards the parking lot. She saw Xavier leaning against his truck looking sexy in blue jeans. It was enough to make her feel warm despite the frigid winter day. She stifled her smile as she walked, not wanting to seem too eager.

"How was your day?" Xavier asked Aria as she approached the truck.

"It was great." she replied. She got in the truck knowing she was teasing him. He was waiting for her answer about Valentine's Day dinner. She couldn't help but smile

"Well," he said, feeling he was being very patient.

Her smile grew, she decided this flirting thing was kind of fun. "Well, I did review my calendar, and it appears I can fit you in." Aria said, trying hard not to start laughing.

He poked her side as she buckled her seatbelt, "very funny."

"Hey, I have to have some fun with you," Aria grinned, losing the battle with laughter.

It was Valentine's Day and a Saturday which made Aria very excited. Xavier was taking her into the city for a fancy dinner. Kiera was coming over to help her with her hair. Kiera was going to go to a more casual place with Gage later.

Aria was settled on the couch watching the snow and the mountains drinking her morning tea when she heard a knock. She got up to let Kiera in.

"Good morning, Dora" Kiera cheerfully greeted her.

Aria rolled her eyes at her cousin. Kiera called Aria Dora often. The name had stuck ever since she had gotten lost in the woods her first week here.

"Ugh, come in." Aria pulled Kiera into the house and shut the large wood door behind her. "It is cold out there."

"That is why my mom, and I got you this!" Kiera exclaimed, pulling a large box out of one of the two large bags she had brought with her.

Aria took the box and walked to the living room. She sat down on the large sectional while starting to tear off the white wrapping paper decorated with gold accented pink and red hearts. She opened the box and pulled out a soft dark green wool cloak with a hood. "Oh, it's gorgeous," Aria exclaimed, standing up, pulling the cloak around her, then spinning in a circle to show it off. "Thank you so much!" Aria was beside herself with gratitude, she bent and hugged her cousin.

"I'm so happy you like it." Kiera smiled. "It is just like a green red riding hood. And it is warm enough for our winters!"

Aria went to look in the mirror, she ran her fingers over the soft wool cloak and the smooth silky inside. She was eager to wear it. She thought her black evening dress with this dark green cloak would make her feel special and beautiful.

Later that day, Aria was dressed, Kiera had left, and Xavier was pulling up in front of Aria's house in a Lincoln town car. "Where did you get the car?" Aria asked, surprised.

"Wow, you look amazing. You know you're supposed to let me knock and walk you out." Xavier grinned at her as he walked around the car. He looked handsome in his dark jeans and red polo shirt.

"Thank you, I know this is a real date and you are trying to be a gentleman, but I am excited to go into the city." Aria grinned back. "You can open my door!"

"It was my grandparent's other car. When they passed away, I decided to keep it." Xavier opened the passenger side door and held out his hand. Aria took Xavier's hand and let him help her into the car. He walked back around and got in the driver's seat. "You really do look amazing."

"Thank you," Aria could feel herself blushing. She had grown close to Xavier ever since she had learned she was a wolf, and while they had snuggled, held hands, and hugged, he had never kissed her.

She had never kissed anyone before and didn't think she had the nerve to make the first move. This was their first real date. She didn't know what to expect. "Have you been to this restaurant before?"

"I have, it seems pasta is one of your favorites so I thought this place would be perfect." Xavier made the turn onto the main road. "Do you like the cloak?"

"I love it" Aria touched the vibrant dark green cloak again. "I was so surprised."

"Did you notice the stitching around the edge?" Xavier asked.

"I did, it looks like little pictures." Aria answered.

"It is, in a way." Xavier smiled at her before slowing for the Elk crossing the road in front of them. "See you can stop for the elk without sliding into the ditch."

"Very funny." Aria rolled her eyes at him, "anyway, what are those pictures?"

"Sorry, I couldn't help myself." He apologized. "Kiera, Katrina, and I looked through all of Cheri's things and found ancient protection glyphs from our ancestors. We all took turns stitching them in." He thought she would think it was a nice gesture, but he was a little concerned she would think they were being overbearing as well. He risked a glance at her when she remained silent. He hadn't expected to see tears rolling over her pale cheeks. "We didn't," He began.

"No, I'm not upset." Aria clarified gently, wiping the tears so that her makeup wouldn't run. "I can't believe you all did this; I'm so grateful." She smiled at him. "Thank you. I wonder why Kiera didn't tell me?"

"She said I could tell you." Xavier wanted Kiera to give the cloak to Aria but also wanted to be a part of the surprise.

"Wait, does this mean they made it?"

"Yes, Kiera didn't tell you?"

"No, I, well I just assumed they bought it." Aria was feeling foolish. "I can't believe I didn't know. I'm going to have to thank both of them again. Can we stop somewhere so I can pick up some thank you cards?"

Xavier loved how kind she was, "There are a few shops we can check out after dinner that have thank you cards and gifts if you want."

"Thank you," As they drove, Aria took in the countryside. They talked about school, the pack, and life in general.

Once they got into the city Aria noticed how different a city was in Montana compared to out east. Cities in the East were tall and close together. Cities in the west seemed larger and more spacious, she thought. After they parked, Xavier had to run around the car so he could open it for Aria before she climbed out. He wanted this to be a special date.

After they ate, they decided to go for a walk to look at some of the nearby shops so Aria could find some thank you cards. As they finished looking at the first shop Aria thought Xavier was being too quiet, "Is everything alright?" Aria asked nervously. She thought it was probably foolish to think so highly of this date since she and Xavier had hung out a lot in the past months, but she felt like this was the first step towards becoming something more than just friends. His quiet demeanor made her worry he wasn't thinking of her as girlfriend material.

"I have been talking to Katrina and Gabriel about the intruders and I think we should all start to look at ALL of our options." Xavier finally told her, putting emphasis on the word all. His words broke into her racing thoughts. "I didn't want to ruin our date with this, but Katrina wants to start tomorrow. I promised her I would see how you felt about it. We have tracked the men down as having come from Eastern Europe around the northern parts of Russia in Siberia."

"What options?" Aria asked.

"Magic options." Xavier looked around to make sure no one was close enough to hear them as they went into another store. "We all needed time to regroup, and we all wanted to make sure you were recovering before we started in on training."

"Who will Katrina learn from?" Aria wondered.

"Katrina found all of Cheri's things and has been looking through some other texts our pack has kept throughout the years." Xavier explained. "Katrina used to practice with your Grandma Cheri, so she knows some magic."

Aria stopped looking through the variety of handmade thank you cards and looked up at him. "I'll study with them." Aria looked around to check for nearby shoppers like Xavier had done before continuing. "I found a couple of totes of my mother's things that we never unpacked in Philadelphia."

"Have you looked through them?" Xavier asked.

"I haven't, I've been afraid to." Aria admitted.

Xavier looked at her big guilt filled eyes and thought he understood how she was feeling. "Aria, don't feel guilty, I have stuff from my mom that I never went through." He reached out to stroke her cheek, "now that I think about it, I should probably see if she had any spell stuff in her belongings as well."

"I feel guilty because I'm angry." Aria told him. "I thought that my mom and I were as close," she sighed, and tears began to form in her eyes, "as close as any two people could be, but it turns out I didn't know her at all."

Xavier wasn't sure he knew the right words to say, "Your mom loved you, she had a reason she left that night, she had a reason she put a spell on you to prevent you from changing. Maybe it's in her things."

"Thanks" Aria squeezed his hand. "I like talking to you. Want to spend the rest of the night looking through totes and boxes and see what we can find?"

He smiled at her," You read my mind."

She smiled back, "Let me get these cards and candles, then we can head back."

Chapter 11

It took them over an hour to grab some boxes from the garage where Xavier had all of his stuff stored and get to Aria's house.

They decided to make tea and set up all of the boxes in the living room. Xavier started a fire after he brought some of Cassie's boxes into the living room from one of the spare bedrooms where Aria kept them. They both started going through the boxes. They sorted things stacking diaries in one pile, keepsake cards in another, and a pile of miscellaneous.

They went through Cassie's diaries first taking turns reading bits and pieces out loud.

Xavier started;

"Today has been amazing. Joel was home for the week, so we took Aria to the beach. She loves the water. I love watching her grow, but I'm sad she is becoming a woman. I will miss her being little."

"Aria and I went to get pedicures today, I love all of the fun girl things I can do with my baby girl."

"It is getting harder to shift. I find the longer I go without shifting the more human I feel. I don't need to shift to live but I do need to keep practicing magic, I have to find something to prevent Aria from shifting, I can tell that I'm running out of time."

"I have found the spell I was looking for to prevent Aria from shifting. I will have to practice more before attempting it. It will prevent her from shifting, only breaking if she is in great need of her wolf. "

'That's why you changed in the woods." Xavier looked at Aria.

"I was in great need of my wolf to protect Kiera." Aria replied using her hands to make air quotations when she said great need.

Xavier kept reading;

"I have been practicing the spell and think it will need a potion to back it up."

"I have done the spell and given Aria the potion. I will have to wait and see if it works, I am slightly worried it will not."

"I can't believe it worked, my precious girl will be safe, she didn't shift with her changing body."

Aria blushed as Xavier read the last section out loud. "I'm going to stock the fire," he got up, giving her time to control her blush, he hadn't meant to embarrass her.

She managed to calm her bright red cheeks by the time Xavier was done stocking the fire. "My turn," Aria said as Xavier sat back down. He didn't say anything, glad the awkward moment had passed.

Aria scanned the page then began reading out loud when she saw a name she recognized;

"I thought I saw Evan in the grocery store today. If he finds me, I will have to move Aria. He cannot find her. He will not take my daughter. She is mine."

"I'm sure Tom and Evan have found me, they tried to follow me home. I will have to be careful. I have no idea what explanation I can give Joel as to why we have to leave our home. I can't stop thinking about the little apartment I lived in with Evan in Portland, after I stupidly went back to him. I think about the white curtains with blue flowers over the sink and the yellow couch we had. I cannot believe I trusted him. If he had not shown his true colors by hitting me, I wouldn't have left in time. He didn't know I was watching when Tom showed up. I think he and Tom planned on taking me somewhere. It was rumored that Tom had been visiting a pack in Eastern Europe."

Aria's head started to spin, she was in shock over what she had just read. "I didn't know that my mom went back to Evan," Aria's eyes filled with tears. "I'm sorry Xavier."

Xavier reached out and pulled her in close, "Aria it doesn't make your mom a bad person we'll have to see if there are earlier journals to see why she went back. We can't know what she was feeling or thinking. It's alright to keep going."

Aria sat back, opened another journal and continued reading bits and pieces;

"I found what I needed in a text I took from my mother when I left. I have placed a confusion spell around the house. I can say the invocation word and they will forget the house and Aria. Unfortunately, it will require a sacrifice, me, to lead them away. Without the sacrifice the spell will not be strong enough and they will be able to find Aria. I hope they do not find us but if they do, I will have to lead them away from Aria, I'm scared I think it will mean they will get me. I don't have enough time to get strong again, I was stupid to stop shifting."

"I am so afraid, I sent a letter to Katrina, I have stayed away for her safety, but I fear they will look for Xavier next. I don't know if Katrina knows Tom and Evan lived that night. Looking back, I'm not sure what happened. When I came back with my spell, I saw Tessa was already dead, Tom looked satisfied and my anger broke. I filled myself with strength from everything around me, I pulled on the life force of everything around me and pushed fear at them. They felt so much pain and their noses were bleeding, they were scared. The spell I used worked. They felt more fear than they had ever felt. They felt pain, they felt they had to leave. When I got over to Tessa there was a small amount of life in her. I had been wrong, she wasn't dead yet. What if my spell took her will to fight? I held her hand and felt her pass completely and the fear I took her will to *live with my spell broke me. On most days I know Tom broke her and she wouldn't have made it. On really bad days I fear my spell took what little life she had left and extinguished it. I look at Aria and think of Tessa's child and feel sick at the thought I took his mother from him. I cannot be sure either way. I left home because I was too afraid to face my parents, my Katrina, Tessa's son, and because I knew that Tom, Evan and the others were not dead, I feared they would come back for retribution. I still don't know how he found me or why I let him convince me to go back to him, but I will never regret my actions as I have Aria and she is my light, my world. I will do everything I can to protect her."*

"I think we've had enough, we both need sleep." Xavier could tell Aria was getting upset. "You, Katrina, Kiera, and Anna are going to study magic and the guys, and I are going to do training drills with groups of the pack. We need to sleep." ,

"I" Aria hesitated trying to find the right words, she felt so comfortable with Xavier, most of the time, but she was embarrassed now, "I had a good time, thank you for dinner."

He reached down and pulled her up. He leaned in and kissed her. The kiss was gentle but powerful. He rested his hands gently on her waist holding himself back from deepening the kiss. "So did I."

She couldn't believe she had just had her first kiss, and she wanted more. She stood on her tiptoes, wrapped her arms around his neck to pull him down to her and kissed him back. Electricity flowed between them, he could feel the need to have her rush through him. He gripped her waist tighter, careful not to hurt her. He separated from her, both their hearts racing. "I, you" Aria couldn't get the words out. She felt like she had been hit by lightning. She sensed he was holding back. Some people would think Xavier was timid and meek, but he was just very aware of his actions and how to control them. He worked very hard to ensure that he didn't lose control. He'd lost so much in his life he wouldn't risk recklessness.

He smiled. "I'll see you in the morning." Aria walked with him to the door. He leaned over and kissed her forehead before walking through the door. He would not rush things, not with Aria.

"Thank you." Aria said as she closed the door and locked it behind him. A forehead kiss always made a person feel cared for.

When she got into the bathroom to wash her face, she felt like a complete idiot. She could not believe she had said thank you. As she checked to make sure everything was set for the night and all the doors were locked she kept replaying the kiss in her head. Once she lay in bed, she kept thinking about how it had felt to kiss Xavier. Then she started to think about how her mother had gone back to that boy, Evan. Evan had contributed to Xavier's mothers death. Did love forgive everything, how could her mother forgive him? Could she forgive Xavier if he did something like that? Her thoughts swirled in her head and at some point, she drifted to sleep.

"Good morning, Aria" Katrina greeted her with a hug. "Xavier told me you two had found some books. I have breakfast all laid out, come on in and we can get started."

Katrina led Aria into the dining room where Kiera and Anna were waiting. Aria handed Katrina and Aria the cards and gifts she had gotten them last night. "You can open them later," Aria said. She wasn't sure how to ask the question she needed to ask, so she just turned to Katrina and blurted it out. "Did you know my mom went back to Evan about 10 months after she left here?

Katrina stood completely still processing the stress in Aria's voice and the actual words she had spoken.

"I'm sorry Katrina, I don't know why she went back. I think I'll find out why if I keep reading her journals, but so far, she hasn't said what convinced her to go back to him." Aria continued.

Katrina grabbed Aria's hands and looked her straight in the eyes, "don't ever be sorry. I loved your mother, she was my other half, she was a good person and I'll never be ashamed of her."

Aria felt relief run through her body. "Xavier said the same thing but I..." Aria trailed off.

"I mean it, Aria. If your mother went back to Evan, it is because she truly believed that he hadn't played a part in Tessa's death." The conviction in Katrina's words allowed Aria to relax further, "Let's eat breakfast and get started." Katrina walked to the table and Aria followed her.

When they finished eating, they poured over the gathered texts whether they were books or diaries, everything that had been kept throughout the ages. While the pack women appeared to stop using magics around the 1920's; it did not appear that any of them stopped collecting data or got rid of the ancient texts they had from their ancestors. There were Celtic texts, and there were texts from Norwegian countries, as well as texts from Romania and Ukraine. The texts spanned across the northern European hemisphere as the pack's ancestors made their way towards the great ice expanse from the green lands of ancient Ireland, where it is believed they came from. They crossed the great ice expanse into Alaska and made their way down to the continental US.

They made piles, intending to scan everything into computer files, so that the history could be preserved if something ever happened to the actual texts. They knew that these texts would hold answers they needed. They each compiled a list of spells they thought would work in protection as well as in self-defense and decided that they would spend the next couple of days compiling. Afterwards they would start researching individual spells and then start practicing. It was important to know which spells were useful. They needed to make sure the spells they used would not require sacrifice. Cassie had been brash and rushed when she used the go away spell that she wrote about in her journal. Their research turned up lots of interesting facts about the pack. They found most of their ancestors had believed that if you held witch blood It was harder to use spells on you, not impossible, but it took a stronger magic user to bespell a witch blood shifter than someone who had very little magic blood in them like Anna. Anna had some witch blood in her and had been able to smell the stranger who had killed Aria's father but not enough to possess the ancient wild scent that encompassed Katrina, Kiera, and Aria.

As the sun started to disappear behind the mountains Katrina said "it's time for a break." They all agreed that they had compiled a lot of texts. The other pack members had been taking turns training throughout the day. Gabriel, Xavier, Gage, Brian, and Chris had another group that were coming to train tomorrow. The day had brought them lots of ideas. Katrina and Kiera wanted to find a way to test to see who possessed witch blood. It appeared that in the past they believed, as they all still did now, that the females were the only ones who could practice magic. It did appear that the witch blood protected the males in the pack as well. Katrina and Kiera thought that they should try and see if Xavier, Gabriel, or Gage could perform magic despite most of the texts saying that it was only a female trait. Just like the males were thought to be the only ones who could turn into brown bears. They thought they should try and see if any of the females with witch blood could change. They realized it was so ingrained that females did magic, and males could shift into multiple forms they never thought to try it the other way around.

"We have a lot to think about and try," Katrina told them as they finished organizing the journals and diaries. "Let's eat some dinner and we can pick this back up after school tomorrow."

Chapter 12

Katrina, Kiera, Anna, and Aria spent every day after school for the rest of the week compiling texts. Gabriel, Xavier, Brian, and Chris spent every day after school training different groups in the pack in combat. They all decided that they would be able to start practicing some actual spells and testing some different theories Saturday morning. The rest of the pack would come in groups starting about midday and they would see who had what abilities.

The week went by fast and soon it was Friday night. They were all sitting around eating pizza and discussing what they had learned after pouring over all of the texts and journals.

"I think Tom is behind the thugs." Xavier blurted out as they were finishing dinner.

Everyone looked at him. "Why do you say that?" Gabriel asked.

"He's right." Aria said.

Xavier nodded, "Aria and I have been going through her mother's journals and we have come up with a timeline." He looked at Aria to make sure she was okay with this.

"Go ahead." Aria nodded.

"It appears that Cassie believed Evan had told Tom that she and Tessa were going back to Cassie's house alone. After Tom hurt my mom, Cassie used an extremely strong and dangerous spell to get them to leave. She lost it when she feared that she may have taken strength from my mom. She was also afraid of Tom and the others coming back for retribution, so she took off. She thought it was the only way to protect herself and her family. It appears she camped and worked as a waitress along the west coast for about 5 or 6 months before Evan got in touch with her. It seems he worked on getting her to come back to him for another 4 or 5 months and she finally believed him and moved in with him in Portland. She was with him for about 4 months." Xavier took a drink of his soda and continued, "From what she wrote things didn't go well after the first couple of weeks. Evan became controlling, and he and Cassie started fighting a lot. Finally, one night Evan hit Cassie when they were arguing and the two of them got into a physical confrontation. Cassie left the apartment and walked around Portland all night. She went to go get her things from the apartment and saw Tom was there talking to Evan. Cassie figured Evan was going to take her to wherever Tom was. She knew he would continue to try to control her. She wrote that Evan had told her Tom was joining a pack in Eastern Europe where they had little rules when it came to regulating abuse and such. She left, never taking any of her things." Xavier looked at Aria.

"She had grabbed a backpack when she left and that had her purse, her money, and a few other items in it. It appears she went to the Loves Truck Stop outside Portland and hitched a ride with a truck driver. She hitched rides all across the country. Finally, she accepted a ride from a young truck driver at a truck stop in Des Moines, Iowa. That young truck driver was my dad." Aria continued the timeline. "She must have gotten pregnant right away. They lived in Philadelphia for a bit, but my mom wanted to move to upstate New York, so by the time I was one year old we were living in our house up there. A little over 12 years later Tom finds her. He searches, and eventually finds our house. He shows up and my mom leaves, casting a forget spell that was so strong it required a sacrifice." Aria's eyes began to tear up. Kiera hugged her and saw Katrina's eyes were starting to tear up as well. "He must have hurt her and then put her in her car and pushed it over the ravine she was found in."

"Joel moves Aria and himself to Philadelphia with Aria's grandmother and Tom never finds them." Xavier continued as Aria began to cry. "Aria and her dad live with Aria's Grandma Ann for about 2 years when she gets sick."

"I had been trying to convince Cassie to come home since I got the letter, she sent warning me that Tom had found her and that he may be after Xavier out for revenge." Katrina picked up the story. "Once I located her in Upper New York state, it was too late, she was gone within 2 days. I asked your dad to let us bury her here after the funeral and he agreed. Shortly after arranging it the letters I sent to Joel began to come back as return to sender. Then with my parents, Xavier's grandparents, and Natasha dying in the car accident I was completely derailed. It took me almost two and a half years to locate Ann's address once I was able to find the strength to search for it again."

"By then Grandma had already passed and Dad and I were at a loss." Aria picked back up, wiping her tears on the Kleenex Gage handed her. "We decided to move here to get to know my mom's family."

"And within weeks of you coming here a strange wolf shows up from Eastern Europe with the ability to block his scent from the typical wolf." Gabriel finished.

Aria and Xavier nodded, "Exactly." They said together.

"So, you think that Tom is the wolf behind all of this." Gage asked.

"It makes sense," Katrina said.

"He hated us." Gabriel added, thinking back to high school. "The city pack has always been envious of us. They are just a normal wolf pack without special abilities. We joke that we're rivals but if it ever came down to a fight, they don't possess our abilities. It was and is rare for our Silver Creek Pack members to date anyone in the Missoula pack. Of course, Tessa and Cassie would be the ones to do things differently. Tom and his family seemed to have a particular jealousy issue when it came to our extra abilities. I think

Tom was hoping he'd be Tessa's mate since she was in the alpha bloodline, he thought he could take over our pack by marrying her."

"I agree," Katrina nodded, "I think that Tom wanted to use the special gifts our pack possesses to gain power."

"I hate him." Xavier growled, "I have never meant him, but I hate him. Why didn't you tell me about him sooner?"

Gabriel and Katrina met Xavier's angry eyes, "We knew you would hate him and didn't want you to grow up with that hate. It was what your grandparents wanted and what they asked us to continue doing if something happened to them."

Xavier sighed, "I guess I can't argue with that."

Gabriel hugged Xavier, "No you can't."

They all smiled at each other letting everyone know they were alright with each other. "We have a lot of work to do tomorrow." Katrina reminded them. "Xavier, you had better get Aria home."

They all bid each other Goodnight. Kiera and Gage walked out with Xavier and Aria.

Gabriel was staring out the window at Kiera, Gage, Aria, and Xavier who were all saying good night again. Tomorrow they would start testing the spells. He looked at his daughter with her purple winter coat standing beside Gage. He knew that Kiera and Gage were growing close. He had thought his daughter becoming interested in a boy would be a day he would live to regret, but he could see that they were taking their time and didn't feel the anger he thought he would. He looked at Aria and Xavier. Aria's dark green coat, blended into Xavier's black coat. He had come to love Aria like another daughter and vowed he would protect her. He had been angry at Cassie for hurting Katrina but none of that was Aria's fault. He admitted to himself that he still blamed himself for Joel's death. He could see that Xavier and Aria were growing closer, especially over the last week. When he searched his emotions, he found that this pleased him as well. Xavier was another son to

Gabriel and would lead the pack someday. He thought Aria would make a great mate and a great co leader.

"What are you thinking about?" Katrina asked, wrapping her arms around his upper chest.

"I'm thinking about how I feel about our baby girl taking a liking to Gage." Xavier told her.

"I like him." Katrina squeezed Gabriel again.

"Me too, and I like Aria and Xavier together as well." Gabriel put his hands over Katrina's. "Sometimes I get mad at Cassie when I think about how she left."

"I know, and I know you don't say anything because she was my twin." Katrina turned him to face her. "Cassie lived with a lot of guilt."

"Do you think that Aria is Evan's child?" Gabriel's question almost made Katrina fall on the floor.

"What, why?" Katrina couldn't even form a coherent sentence.

"Maybe she isn't, but damn Katrina, the timeline is so tight. Cassie could have been pregnant when she left Portland.' Gabriel steadied her, "I think it is rare for a half blood wolf to be so strong."

"I can't think about it right now." Katrina put her hands on his cheeks, and stared into his dark eyes so he could see the pleading in hers "Can we please deal with that question another day?"

He smiled at her, softening his eyes so she would relax. "Sure, let's go get some sleep before you, Kiera, Aria, and Anna use us as test subjects."

Katrina let him lead her upstairs, but she didn't think she would get any sleep thinking about what repercussions they were going to face because of their past.

The next morning Katrina, Aria, Kiera, and Anna lined up each of the guys across the family room three feet apart. They had moved all of the furniture into the living room, so they had space.

"It's too bad it wasn't a bit warmer" Kiera mourned looking outside. "We could practice outside."

Katrina patted her daughter's head. "Alright, we each have a spell we are going to try on you." she said, turning to the five test subjects. "Some of them will affect you, some of them will be self-protection spells."

"We are not going to tell you what we are trying until you tell us how it felt." Kiera explained.

"That way you will not have any preconceived ideas of what you should have felt." Aria continued.

"And since Aria, Kiera, and Katrina have a lot more witch blood in them than me, we are going to have one of them and me try the same spell to see if it is more or less effective." Anna concluded.

"Any Questions?" Katrina asked.

All of them shook their heads no. They all looked slightly afraid. "Alright Xavier, Gage, and Brian go in the other room, so we can try a spell out multiple times with no preconceived ideas." Once they had left Katrina held up her hands and shouted "Confuzie!" at Chris with no warning.

Her son instantly had a blank look on his face. "What are we doing?" Chris asked looking around, "What happened to the furniture?"

"Chris what is today?" Kiera asked.

"Uhm, I don't know," he turned to Gabriel, "Dad what's wrong with me?"

"Anula Confuzie" Katrina shouted as she raised her hand at Chris again.

His face cleared and he looked around. "Are you alright?" Katrina asked him, concerned for her son. Maybe they shouldn't be using each other as test subjects. Except Gabriel was certain they needed to practice in order to be able to perform spells during a confrontation when the pressure would be high, and their actions would need to be second nature.

"I'm fine mom," Chris assured her, "it just took a second for everything to come back to me. It was like I lost time. I..."

Before Chris could continue Anna raised her arms and yelled. "Confuzie"

Chris paused and looked around. "What was I saying?"

"Anula Confuzie" Anna shouted the reversal as Katrina had done.

Everyone gave Chris a few moments to recover. "Wow," Chris exclaimed, "I can totally tell the difference between the practitioners. Mom's spell was strong, and I don't remember anything, Anna's spell just made me forget the thread of my conversation."

"Good, this is good." Katrina said as Aria took notes. "This is the type of information we need. Go tell Xavier and Brian to come in. Remember, do not tell them anything."

"I know mom," Chris muttered as he walked out of the family room.

As Brian and Xavier walked in the room, Kiera shouted, "Confuzie" giving them no time to process.

Both of them stopped and looked around, "What happened to the furniture mom?" Brian asked.

"I know we were practicing something, but I cannot figure out what." Xavier said. "Maybe we were just supposed to do homework?"

"Anula Confuzie" Aria shouted this time.

Their faces cleared. "How do you feel?" Katrina asked.

"It felt like I was in a fog," Xavier said.

"Me too," Brian confirmed.

"Confuzie," Anna shouted. Brian and Gabriel turned and looked at her.

"Umm" Brian hesitated, "I don't feel anything,"

"Me either." Xavier added.

"It only tripped up Chris a bit, but it did affect him." Anna told them, "I wonder why Brian and Chris are not affected the same way, they are twins."

"I want you to say the undo spell just in case." Katrina said to Anna.

"Anula Confuzie." Anna shouted.

"Thank you, Anna," Gabriel smiled at her as she stepped forward. "Chris, Gage, come in here." He shouted.

When Chris and Gage entered the room Gabriel began, "Chris said Katrina's confusion spell made him black out and Anna's spell just made him lose the thread of the conversation he was having. Xavier and Brian knew they were supposed to be doing something but couldn't remember what when Kiera put the confusion spell on them. They felt nothing with Anna's confusion spell." He took a sip of water and continued, "Brian is a healer, even though he and Chris are twins I think that is affecting his reaction. Xavier has alpha and witch blood so I think he will always be harder to spell."

"I agree." Katrina said. "Let's try some more."

They tried a go away spell, milder than the one that Cassie had used that fateful night all those years ago. They tried a fall spell, a feel cold spell, and a sad spell. As they spelled each other they realized they could draw on inner strength or draw strength from other living things. Katrina thought they needed to look into this more and see if it caused harm, even if they pulled energy in small doses.

"I'm starting to feel the connection between drawing on energy sources and using internal strength," Aria told them as they sat for a break and to eat lunch. "I can see how my mom's spell would have been so strong if she pulled on multiple life sources including people."

"I think we will need to keep our strength up and be cautious, so we don't overdo it or take too much from others." Katrina said.

"I hope we are not opening Pandora's box." Gabriel thought out loud.

"Don't worry Dad, we will be careful." Kiera gestured to Aria, "we saved one of the best spells for last, and Aria is really good at it."

"For the afternoon we will need to go outside, I think it's best if you guys are in your wolf form," Katrina finished her last bite. "Next weekend I'd like to test all the spells again with all of you in your wolf and bear forms, we need to know the extent of what we can do here. If we don't know who we are spelling we can't use the confusion, go away, or fall spells. We can't be sure they will work. We need to go with personal self-defense magic that will work on anyone."

After they finished eating, they all got ready to go outside. Gabriel, Gage, Brian, Chris, and Xavier all shifted before they went outside. Katrina, Kiera, Anna, and Aria bundled up in winter gear. "Okay" Katrina said once they were in the backyard, "I want you guys to come at us like you are going to attack us. We are going to try and protect ourselves with a physical barrier. You need to try and get past it if you can."

Chapter 13

They stood on opposite sides of the yard. The wolves started towards Karina, Kiera, Aria, and Anna. All four of them shouted "proteja pe mine." With the words a translucent barrier formed surrounding each of them individually. The barrier shimmered in the light. They could all see that Kiera's, Aria's, and Katrina's spells were much stronger than Anna's spell. All of them could get through Anna's barrier but it was thick as if they were walking through thick mud. No one could penetrate Kiera's, Katrina's, or Aria's barriers. "This is fantastic." Katrina smiled, "this is what we need to keep practicing."

"It takes quite a bit of energy." Kiera huffed out letting her barrier drop.

"Yeah, I can see where we have to be strong to hold it for any length of time." Aria added, dropping her barrier as well. "It may be that we have to start working it like any muscle. We also have to figure out how to take just a little bit of life force from each thing like grass and trees.

"We need to keep ourselves strong, well fed, and healthy. The magic we're using isn't to harm others so we shouldn't be hurting the grass and trees by pulling on their life forces, but we will definitely need to check into this more." Katrina told them all.

"Now that we've tried spells on you, are you all up for trying to spell us?" Katrina asked. "I think we should try the confusion and protection spells followed by the barrier spell.

The females tried to explain what it felt like to do a spell. Kiera explained, "you have to kind of reach deep inside yourself. Pull out the feeling you need. Like if you want the person to go away, you have to feel very strongly that you want them to go away. If you want to confuse the person, you have to think of them being confused. Hold that feeling within you until it becomes a really strong feeling, then push it at the person you want to spell as you say the words of intent." Kiera looked around. "I don't know, maybe everyone's going to have to start meditating to connect with each part of their body. If we can strengthen our connection we may eventually be able to spell as wolves. Right now, we need the additional intention of saying it out loud. But I'm guessing that we could all learn to do the spells as our animals, once we no longer need the additional force of speaking the spells out loud."

Katrina looked at her daughter, "I think you're right we shout and put our hands up right now because we need those extra gestures to energize the spell. I think if we can learn to center ourselves through meditation learning to really tune into our bodies and surroundings, we will be able to do these spells in our animal form."

"I wonder if I could do it as a wolf now with me being so new to it?" Aria thought out loud.

"I think that we should try casting spells as wolf's next week." Katrina said. "We're all pretty tired, let's have each of you," she turned towards the males, "try the proteja pe mine spell and the confusion spell and we'll go from there."

Each of them took their turns with the confusion spell. "Confuzie," Gabriel shouted at his wife.

Katrina shook her head to clear an uncomfortable feeling. "I felt the magic touch me, but I don't feel confused. I feel like it just brushed me. It is a very strange feeling."

Gabriel tried it on everyone in turn. Both Kiera and Aria felt the same as Katrina; it was like they were just being brushed with the magic, but it had no effect. Anna did feel confused with the spell, but it was not as strong as when she had been spelled by Katrina. Chris, Brian, Gage, and Xavier all tried with similar results. Chris and Brian's magic was so weak Kiera, Katrina, and Aria barely felt a brush. Anna felt a stronger brush but the spell itself did not work. Gage and Xavier's spells brushed everyone stronger and even mildly confused Anna.

"I think I understand," Katrina exclaimed. They all turned and looked at her, "I think that the reason they don't think males can do magic is because they were always trying out their spells on the females. We can do magic on witch males but because the females have the stronger magic in their blood the males can't bespell witch born females. So, they assumed the men couldn't do magic. They probably never even tried to have the men spell non magic pack members.

"That sounds right. Plus, why wouldn't you have the men shift to bear and wolves if their strength was fighting." Gabriel added.

"I think you're right, that's the only explanation that makes sense." Kiera agreed. "Maybe we can shift to the brown bear." There was pure excitement in Kiera's voice.

"Don't you like your little wolf?" Gage teased.

Kiera glared at him, "My wolf is not small and of course I like my wolf, but it would be so awesome to shift into both forms." Gabriel tried to smother his grin before his daughter saw it. Katrina poked him in the ribs. Gage gave Gabriel away by glancing at him. "You all better be nice to me," Kiera warned. "I'm a strong magic user, and if I can shift into both forms, I'll be a total badass." She turned and marched into the house.

"I'm a little afraid." Xavier grinned.

"You had better be." Aria threatened poking him in the arm and going after her cousin.

"Okay now that you have irritated them let's all take a break. We will need our rest for tomorrow. Let's all go inside and make dinner." Katrina looked at each of them in turn daring any of them to continue with the comments and followed behind Aria.

"You're the alpha Dad," Chris pointed out.

"Where have you been living the last 16 years?" Gabriel asked ruffling his son's hair, "I may be the male alpha, but she is the female alpha and my mate. Everyone knows that makes her the real one in charge."

"Would you argue with mom?" Brian pointed out.

"No" Chris, Gage, and Xavier answered in unison. They all walked into the house laughing.

After dinner, Kiera, Gage, and Xavier went home with Aria. They were going to watch a movie and sleep over in the living room.

The guys lit a fire while Aria and Kiera found a movie. They were all on the couch watching a movie when Aria realized she didn't know as much about Gage as she thought she should. "Do you know where your mother was from?" Aria asked him. She could remember hearing she was from a different country.

"Yes, she was from Romania." Gage turned towards Aria. "Her pack moved to Siberia when she was ten."

"How did she get to the states?" Aria wondered.

"Her father had died when she was five. Two years after they migrated into Siberia her mother met another male shifter." Gage balled his hand into a fist, "he was a bad man. No one would listen to my mom, so she ran away. She was only fifteen years old."

"Oh, Gage, I'm sorry you don't have to talk about it." Aria sat up, "I didn't know."

"It's alright," Gage reassured her, "It's hard but you should know." Kiera was rubbing Gage's back as he continued. "She made it to Seattle, Washington with a fake Id and passport. She started waitressing and met a wolf. Within a month she got pregnant with me and realized he too was a bad man. She never went into details, but it sounds like he was violent."

"Oh, that's awful." Aria knew her sentiment wasn't enough.

"She never told him she was pregnant, she left and went to Spokane." Gage continued, "She had me there. She worked as a waitress and rented a small apartment. She was there until I was about two years old, then decided to move further east to Missoula. She found another small apartment and found another job as a waitress. She had only been there a week when Cheri came in."

"Our Grandma." Kiera reminded Aria.

"I remember."

"Cheri convinced my mom within a month to move up here and live. She worked at Doc's as a receptionist and we rented the apartment over the garage at your grandparent's house, well this house." Gage smiled. "She was amazing. She fit in great with the pack. She became good friends with Katrina, she took classes online to learn to be a nurse to help Doc. She helped people."

"She does sound amazing." Aria agreed.

"I miss her every day." Gage confessed. "As you know she was in the car with your grandparents when they went over the cliff."

"Thank you for telling me about her." Aria didn't know what else to say but she was grateful that she had asked.

The next morning, they gathered on the lawn at Katrina's and Gabriel's house. "I really want to go first." Kiera whispered to Anna and Aria.

"Be patient." Aria told her. Aria was a bit nervous, she was still learning everything she could about her wolf. She loved the freedom and the power she felt running through the woods. She was amazed that Keira was so excited.

"Okay ladies, you had your fun with us yesterday. It's our turn." Gabriel addressed them as though he were teaching a class. "We are going to see if you guys can shift into brown bears. We have been discussing how the bear feels compared to the wolf. We all feel that the wolf is a deep part of us and the brown bear is extra, almost like the wolf is playing dress up."

Anna laughed interrupting Gabriel, "Sorry" she said when Gabriel looked at her. "It was funny to hear you say 'playing dress up'." She looked sheepish.

Gabriel smiled at her, so she knew he was not mad and continued, "Xavier, Gage, Chris, Brian explain to them how it feels to you when you shift to bear."

"I call up my inner bear by thinking of cozy caves in the winter and snuggling in with a full belly." Gage said first. Everyone looked at him surprised like maybe he was still out of it from one of the confusion spells. "What? I have a softer side." Gage said, defending himself.

"I feel the power, the sheer size and strength of the bear. I also feel the bears wisdom." Xavier said going next, still grinning from everyone finding out about Gage's thoughts on his bear. .

"Oh sure, no one is surprised at his answer." Gage muttered.

"I picture meadows where bears graze, eating sedge grass, and napping in the sun." Brian shared.

"I picture the salmon running and fishing as a bear," Chris added.

"Good" Gabriel praised them, "I think of the bear's strength and power. I think of its ability to protect its territory. I feel the fierceness of the bear, and like Xavier I feel its wisdom." He paused and looked around. "Any questions?" Everyone shook their heads no. "Alright, Kiera, go for it." Xavier said, waving her forward.

Kiera stepped forward as her dad stepped back. She stood in the brilliant light of the day with patches of snow and brown grass surrounding her from the last warm spell. She thought of what each of them had said. She thought of the power of the bear, the bear fishing, she waited, feeling an earthiness begin to rise within her. She briefly thought of teddy bears which almost made her laugh and lose her concentration. She bore down on her concentration and thought of the bear's paws, suddenly she felt it, it was faint, but it was there. She felt it grow inside of her until she realized she was a bear. She was absolutely delighted with it. She played around the yard a bit, eventually settling down to watch the others.

Anna stepped forward at Gabriel's gesture. She stood there thinking of all the things the others had told her. She thought about cubs, dens, meadows, fishing, and even the size, strength, and power of the bear. She stood there for over double the time it had taken Kiera to shift. She thought she could feel a faint tingle, but it never grew. "I think I feel it faintly, but I can't get it to rise." Anna said, sounding defeated.

"That's alright we will keep practicing," Gabriel reassured Anna with a hug. "Maybe it will just take more practice to develop and find your inner bear." He turned to Katrina, "Alright kitty it's your turn."

Katrina smiled "you guys better hope I can't shift into a brown bear."

"The ultimate Mama bear." Brian laughed.

Katrina thought of the strength of the mother bear. The way the mama bears will take on larger male bears to protect their young. She thought of protecting her daughter from the strangers who wanted to take her. She thought of someone hurting any of her children and much quicker than it had been for Kiera she stood as a bear.

"Wow" Chris exclaimed "Mom, look at you!"

Katrina snuffed at him and lumbered over to lay by her daughter.

"Alright" Xavier turned to Aria, "your turn."

Aria closed her eyes and at first felt panicked picturing the bear that had attacked her and Kiera. She pushed the fear aside and began to think of a brown bear walking a mountain path, swimming in a stream, tracking scents, playing with cubs. She thought she felt a sensation that was different from the sensation that comes before shifting to a wolf, but she wasn't sure. She dug deeper to think of the earth dens that were used for hibernation. She thought of a bear standing on its hind legs warning those that dared to threaten it. She . pictured what it would have been like to stand tall and protect her father and her father. Suddenly, she was the bear.

"Amazing." Gage said.

Katrina and Kiera came up alongside her. Giving her comfort.

All of them felt amazing, "Anna shift to wolf and come with us." Gabriel told her, "We are going to all run as bears and get them acquainted with this form."

"Is it alright if I shift to wolf with Anna?" Brian asked.

"Absolutely," Gabriel said.

After the others shifted, seven bears and two wolves spent the day out in the mountains. They played in the snow, chased Elk and Mule deer. They were all exhausted when they made it back home. Everyone met in the kitchen after showering and changing.

"I don't think I have the energy to make dinner." Katrina sat down on the stool at the breakfast bar attached to the counter and looked at Gabriel.

"Don't look at me, I am too exhausted to cook." Gabriel held his hand up seeing the look on Katrina's face. "But, I'm not too tired to drive," he looked at Xavier, "How about you?"

"I'm not too tired to drive," Xavier said, "what did you have in mind?"

"Let's all go out to eat." Gabriel decreed, "We can go to the steak house on Hwy 2 just outside of town."

"That sounds wonderful." Katrina smiled.

"That does sound great!" Kiera hugged her dad. "Good idea Dad."

"I don't think I can even make it to the car," Aria moaned. "You've all been running around as wolves for years. I don't think I'm in as good of shape as all of you."

They all chuckled and Xavier walked over to her. "Well," he said, giving no other indication of his intentions, he bent down and scooped her up over his shoulder, "I guess I'll have to carry you."

"Umph" Aria's breath escaped out partly from Xavier's shoulder pressing on her stomach and partly from laughing.

"This is not what I meant." Aria finally got out.

"I'll grab her shoes." Kiera said from behind Aria and playfully smacked her cousin on the butt.

Katrina, Chris, Brian, and Anna climbed into Gabriel's vehicle, while Kiera and Gage climbed into Xavier's vehicle. Xavier set Aria in the passenger seat of his vehicle. They drove to the restaurant as the sun set. The moon was bright and reflected off the snow that still covered the ground. The white snow reflecting the bright moon turned the night into a permanent twilight rather than a true dark.

They all enjoyed their meal talking, laughing, getting their minds off of death, magic, shifting, self-defense, and all of the stress of the past that had come back to haunt them. Two hours had passed before they were finished.

"I forgot my cell phone on the table." Kiera realized as they were all getting into their respective vehicles. "I'll just be a minute." Kiera started to walk back inside, turning back she called, "I have to use the bathroom quickly too."

"You can go ahead," Xavier told Gabriel, "We'll wait for her and be right behind you."

Gabriel didn't think it would hurt anything to get going, after all there were four of them together. Including two very strong witch blood females as well as the pack's future Alpha and Beta. "Alright, see you at home, let me know if you all drop Aria off first."

"Will do." Xavier said standing by the driver's side door.

"She'll probably get inside and realize it was in her pocket the whole time." Gage laughed, "she does that all the time."

"She does not." Aria defended her cousin, "Plus you shouldn't tease her when she's not here to defend herself" Aria stuck her tongue out at Gage.

"Oh, come on, I was only teasing." They all started to laugh when Kiera came out of the restaurant at a faster pace than they expected. Gage and Xavier stiffened, "something is wrong" Gage started towards Kiera as Aria turned around to see her.

"Go" Kiera said, pointing at the vehicle, walking very quickly but not running so she did not attract attention.

"What's going on?" Gage asked.

"Get in the car, start driving, I'll explain." Kiera said under her breath.

Aria's belly tightened as Kiera and Gage climbed in the back seat and Xavier got into the driver's seat. "Explain," Xavier commanded as he started out of the parking lot.

"I think that Glen was in there with the two thugs and another man." Kiera told them.

"Men came around the back of the building and got into a car as Kiera was coming out. Now a car is starting to pull out behind us," Gage was still looking around. "Xavier, should I call Gabriel?"

"What if they catch us?" Aria asked fear spreading through her body squeezing her chest. The men who killed her father may be following them, she thought she was going to stop breathing as her chest tightened further in panic.

"Call Gabriel" Xavier was watching the vehicle behind them and thought it was speeding up to close the gap.

"It's okay Aria." Kiera put her hands on Aria's shoulder, "You are strong, feel your wolf, feel your bear, feel your magic. You are strong, you can defend yourself, you can help us defend each other." Aria tried to focus on her cousin's words as they penetrated Aria's fear. Aria started to take deep breaths searching inside herself for her wolf. Kiera continued, "Feel your wolf's anger at its pack being threatened. Feel your wolf's anger at a trespasser on your territory. Feel your wolf rise to defend." As Kiera spoke, she felt her own eyes shift.

"Your eyes." Gage was staring at Kiera, "Holy cow, Kiera, your eyes are glowing."

"Do you feel it Aria," Kiera asked.

Aria felt the fear leave her as her wolf rose up and growled. "Yes, I am wolf, I am magic, I am strong. They will not take any more of my family. They will not threaten me." She felt power start to flow between her cousin and herself.

"What is happening?" Xavier asked, trying not to be distracted from the flow of power connecting Kiera and Aria.

"We are sharing power." Aria whispered, not wanting to break her concentration.

Gage had dialed everyone in the other car, and no one had answered. He kept trying as he turned to see the car right behind them, and another car behind the one following them. He tried Gabriel's cell phone again, this time Gabriel answered. "Gabriel, turn around, we are being followed and I think they're going to try and run us off the road. If they do, we won't be driving so look for us on the side of the road. I got to go." Gage spoke quickly and hung up as the car rear ended them.

Gabriel hit the brakes and did a U-turn in the middle of the road. "What's wrong?" Katrina asked.

"They are being tailed. They think the car tailing them is going to try and run them off the road." Gabriel smothered his anger, finding his calm, he thought better when he suppressed the anger.

"They will protect each other, we will get to them." Katrina reassured everyone in the car as well as herself. "She would not lose anyone else.

"As soon as we find them, I'll pull over, Anna and Brian shift to wolf when we find them, Chris and I will shift to bear, Katrina stay human and use any of the spells you are confident will work."

Xavier fought to keep the SUV on the road. "Hang on." He yelled. Thinking fast he said, "I'm going to pull over. We are less likely to get hurt fighting outside the car than getting run off the side of a cliff."

"I agree" Gage said, "As soon as you stop, I will get out and shift to bear."

"I'll shift to wolf." Xavier prepared to stop at a small rest stop about a mile up the road. The car rear ended them again. Xavier had slowed down so the hit did not cause the vehicle to lose control. "There is a second vehicle following us, be prepared for anything. I'm not sure if Gabriel will get back in time."

"Aria and I will stay human and use our magic if needed." Kiera and Aria worked to dampen the glow between them.

"Take my hand as soon as we are out, we are stronger together." Aria squeezed Kiera's hand.

Xavier took the entrance to the wayside a little quicker than normal but did not lose control of the vehicle when it fish tailed. They all jumped out as the vehicle pulled in tight behind them, stopping inches behind their car.

Aria and Kiera were holding hands with a bear on one side of them and a wolf on the other when the men climbed out of the car. One of the thugs sneered at them, "Think you can protect your women, little boys."

Xavier growled and Gage roared, the men stopped accessing the situation as they noticed Aria and Kiera's hair floating on the calm night and the dripping light flowing between their hands.

"Let the little ladies come with us and nobody gets hurt." Glen said, stepping in front of the thugs. The sight before him was magnificent but he had seen his alpha destroy magic just like it.

Xavier growled louder as three other men and a woman who had gotten out of the second car, walked up behind the four strangers. "What the hell are you doing?" A tall muscular man, with dark eyes and dark hair asked.

"Stay out of this." One of the thugs commanded never looking at the group. "We have business with these little females."

Kiera recognized the man who had spoken and smiled. Relief and disappointment flooded through her when she realized they would not have to test their new found skills tonight.

Xavier growled again and Gage roared but they did not charge the strangers, they too had recognized the newcomers.

"Well, you see," the dark haired man continued, "We don't think the alpha would appreciate you taking his daughter."

Chapter 14

One of the thugs turned to the group, finally deciding ignoring them would not work. "You don't want to mess with us." The thug reached into his pocket as he spoke. The woman next to the dark-haired man did a roundhouse kick knocking the thug and the gun he was reaching for to the ground. There was a moment of silence and then all hell broke loose. Two of the trespassers went after the newcomers while two of them went for Kiera and Aria. Xavier and Gage advanced, putting themselves in front of Aria and Kiera. One of the trespassers had a gun, "Stay back he warned, and no one gets hurt."

Another vehicle screeched into the wayside at a high rate of speed, the trespasser with the gun was distracted for a moment and Xavier pounced, knocking him to the ground. Instinctively Xavier went for his throat, but the trespasser protected himself and Xavier ended up with his mouth around the man's arm.

Gabriel, Chris, Brian, Anna, and Katrina came up fast feeling relief seeing Gage, Xavier, Kiera, and Aria were still standing. Brian, Anna, and Katrina surrounded Aria and Kiera, while Chris and Gabriel went to help Gage and Xavier. A gun shot rang out causing everyone to freeze. The trespassers used the distraction to get in their car and take off.

Gabriel shifted and ran to the three newcomers surrounding one of their group that was on the ground. "How bad?"

"It just grazed me." The dark haired man tried to sit up.

"Let me look at it," The woman insisted, pushing him back to the ground to prevent him from rising.

"I'm fine, don't fret." He told her, pushing her back a bit so he could rise to his feet.

Everyone else walked up to them. "Thank you." Gabriel reached his hand out to shake the dark haired man's hand.

"We were pulling in when we saw your girl walking fast to the car looking afraid," he explained to Gabriel, "then we saw these men rush out and follow them out of the parking lot. Sarah said it didn't feel right and thought we should follow your pups."

"We are grateful." Xavier stepped forward shaking all of their hands.

"You are a kick ass fighter in human form, Sarah." Kiera said in awe of her.

Sarah smiled. "Thank you. But he was slow."

"This is Cory Alpha of the pack to the west of us by Coeur de Alene, his mate Sarah, his beta Jim, and Jim's son Phil. Jim and Cory grew up with us" Gabriel introduced them to Aria, "This is Aria Cassie's daughter."

"Nice to meet you," Sarah shook Aria's hand. "You look just like your mother."

"Thank you," Aria smiled, "and thank you for helping us tonight."

"We are grateful for your intervention." Katrina surprised Sarah by hugging her. "If you ever need anything, call, I mean it."

Sarah returned the hug," I will, I don't have kids, but I understand how precious they are."

They all got into their vehicles and headed home. Gabriel followed Xavier. They all made it to the main house.

"I'm going to bring Aria home and sleep on the couch," Xavier told the others as they got out.

"Call me when you get there and are inside with the doors locked." Gabriel told them. "We will reconvene in the morning and discuss what happened."

"Be careful," Katrina warned them, "I don't think they will attempt to come at us again tonight, but don't let your guard down."

"We won't take any chances," Aria reassured her.

Katrina hugged both Xavier and Aria before they got back into the SUV.

Xavier started to pull out, "Wait" Aria said. She rolled down her window. "Katrina, can you call the school tomorrow and let them know I won't be in, I need to rest."

Katrina gave her a sympathetic look, "Absolutely, we need to make sure we are taking care of ourselves."

Aria and Xavier drove to Aria's house in silence. Xavier walked around and opened Aria's door. She sat for a minute then took the hand he was holding out. "I don't feel like I can keep doing this." Aria confessed.

Xavier looked at her. "Tonight, we just have to be, they won't come at us on our own territory yet, I just feel it." He stepped into the opening of the car door and pulled her into him. "We will get through this." Xavier picked her up, shut the door and carried her towards the house.

"If I was a strong independent woman I would be walking on my own." Aria said, laying her head on his shoulder.

"You are strong." Xavier reassured her. "When your mother died you didn't break, when your grandmother died you didn't break, when your father died you didn't break, when you shifted unexpectedly you didn't break. You are a rock, you have been strong. Part of being strong means knowing when to take a break and knowing who to lean on." Xavier unlocked the door and walked in, sitting her on the large wooden bench just inside the door.

"I guess but it seems like everyone only values independent strength," Aria told him, taking off her shoes. "It's like leaning on others or taking a break isn't considered strength. Like to be a strong woman you can't count on a man to have your back."

"I agree that is how a lot of people portray strength, but I think that is a kind of strength that eventually bends and breaks." Xavier locked the door behind him. "I'm going to start a fire."

Aria smiled at him, "I'm going to take a quick shower and change."

When she got up to the bathroom, she looked at herself in the mirror, "Who are you?" she said to her own reflection. She thought she had a lot to learn about herself, but Xavier was right, she needed to let herself heal, let herself trust others, that was true strength. She took a quick shower and put on her pajamas.

When she got back down stairs Xavier had a fire going and her favorite honey herbal mint and raspberry tea on the coffee table. She smiled at him, "Thank you."

"Can I shower quickly?" Xavier asked her.

"Of course." Aria said.

Xavier ran out to his truck and grabbed a backpack he kept in it with a change of clothes. While he showered Aria sipped her tea, enjoyed the fire, and got her TV playlist ready. Aria loved watching two women on YouTube. One woman, Hannah Lee Duggan was a beautiful model who chopped her own wood, remodeled her house, and did all sorts of remodeling and redecorating on her own. Aria wanted to be as independent and clever as her. She also wanted to dress like her. The other built her own tiny house, chopped her own wood, made music, cooked really yummy looking food, and always found joy in nature. She wanted to share her joy in these channels with Xavier and was excited that he was sitting down to watch these channels with her for the first time.

He came out of the bathroom in navy blue sweatpants and a white T-shirt. "Do you need anything else?" Xavier asked Aria. He loved seeing her cuddled up on the couch in a quilt she had told him her grandma Ann made.

"I'm good, thank you again for the tea." Aria smiled at him, "I have my YouTube playlist ready."

Xavier returned her smile, "I'd love to watch it with you." He walked over and sat next to her. They snuggled on the couch and began to watch the Hannahleedugan channel.

"I don't know, I think you are going to have to reassess." Xavier looked at Aria.

"What?" Aria asked, confused.

"Hannah is cutting firewood with a fever." Xavier paused his grin, growing wider. "In a dress. I'm impressed."

Aria started to laugh, "Hey, you don't wear a dress either and you use a log splitter."

Xavier was laughing so hard at her indignant look he couldn't respond.

Aria woke up in her bed having no memory of getting there. The last thing she remembered Hannah had been cleaning her cottage. She got up and decided to get dressed before going downstairs. Halfway down the stairs dressed in sweatpants and a T-shirt, she smelled breakfast and heard voices. She was pleasantly surprised to see Xavier, Kiera, and Gage in her kitchen making breakfast.

"This is a pleasant surprise." Aria told them walking into the room.

Kiera gave her the menu "Gage is making his famous blueberry pancakes, Xavier is making his famous hashbrowns, and they have bacon."

"Don't forget my famous iced Caramel mochas" Gage reminded her, setting down an amazing smelling drink in front of Aria as she sat down.

"It all looks and smells delicious!" Aria said before taking a sip of the delicious coffee drink. "I thought you would all be in school."

"Mom and Dad decided we all needed a break," Kiera explained.

"We have an itinerary for today." Xavier explained.

"We are going to finish breakfast and go for a run together as the animal of your choice." Gage told her.

"It is supposed to storm this afternoon," Xavier continued, "so after our run we are going to veg out and finish catching up on your favorite YouTube channels."

"Then we are going to eat dinner, play some games or something and go to bed." Kiera finished.

"Wow, that sounds like the perfect day." Aria smiled, "thank you."

"We need to make sure we don't wear ourselves out." Gage explained.

They went out into the yard and shifted. They all choose to run as wolves. They ran straight to the north edge of their territory, thinking if the intruders were still around, they would not be that far north. They were all wary of their surroundings and while the run was enjoyable it lacked the pure joy it had had before they realized the strange wolves were going to keep coming after them. The strange wolves had a personal vendetta. Xavier kept pushing down the feelings of guilt that tried to overwhelm him at the thought that it was his father causing all of these problems. They ran through the snow easily staying on top, they could see other animals had punched through the top layer of snow and sunk in. The day was cool but did not feel cold. Their thick dense coats and the exertion of the run kept them warm. They collapsed in a pile midway up a mountain. They lay, relaxing their muscles but not their senses. All of them felt it at the same time, a tingle of the senses. They jumped to their feet and looked around. They felt like they were being watched. Xavier started back towards home Aria and Kiera following him, Gage bringing up the rear. They were almost back inside the Silver Creek township border when 5 wolves jumped in front of them. Xavier paused, keeping himself between Aria and Kiera and the strangers. Gage shifted from wolf to brown bear and held his position behind them. The strange wolves were shocked to see how seamless the rear wolf shifted to his bear form. They started to approach, sure they could take the two females. They had been instructed not to hurt the two young male wolves. In their opinion this made the task harder but not impossible, after all they were just kids. Both sides were preparing to fight when both sides felt a hum of power. Twelve wolves came out of the far side of the clearing. They were stalking forward, their eyes on the five strange wolves. Aria and Kiera could sense the attention of all twelve of the wolves. They instinctively knew that the wolves, who were actual wolves not shapeshifters, would not hurt them. The twelve wolves wound their way around Gage brushing up against him even in his bear form. They made their way up past Aria and Kiera the white wolf who was the alpha brushing along Aria's side. All of the wolves except one grey wolf moved up to Xavier. The white wolf stopped when he came up to Xavier' silver grey wolf and howled. Xavier bowed to the alpha and then sang with him. Aria, Kiera, and Gage joined in. The five trespassers' were not quite sure what to do.

When they had finished singing the white wolf passed Xavier, all but a black wolf followed their alpha and stopped between the five strangers and Xavier, Gage, Aria, and Kiera. The white wolf snarled, the rest started to growl a warning. The five strangers were afraid.

While the other wolves were confronting the would-be abductors, the light grey and black wolves who had stayed behind started nudging Xavier, Aria, and Kiera. Gage shifted back to wolf and getting the idea all four of them followed the grey and black wolves.

They ran through an untouched part of the forest instead of the way they normally went. When Xavier and Gage tried to go the way, the path led the black wolf snapped at them pushing them the other way. Kiera and Aria followed without hesitation sensing that the wolves were trying to get them home safely.

The strange wolves turned and ran as the real wolf pack advanced on them. Even the thugs weren't up to taking on ten wolves who had to fight nature every day to survive. The wolf pack ran after their queries close on their heels but never catching them. They were content to chase them out of their territory. The trespassers ran, making it to the spot where their other three companions were waiting with a vehicle. The wolf pack stopped in the tree line, the white wolf instinctively knowing not to expose himself or his pack. The three reinforcements that had shown up after the fight the previous night held rifles at the ready after seeing their companions running in fear. The five shifted and said "let's get out of here we'll explain what happened on the way." Confused but sensing their urgency they all got in the van and took off.

Xavier, Aria, Kiera and Gage would've run right into the three men with guns had they not followed the light grey and black wolves. The grey and black wolves took them about a half mile around the men with guns. The white wolf took the rest of his pack across Silver Creek and met them about 15 miles from Gabriel and Katrina's home. Aria, Kiera, and Gage felt a tingle of excitement as the rest of the pack joined them. None of them had ever run with real wolves. Their joy returned. They were not afraid. They were not leery. They were just wolves. They matched their stride to their wild brethren and let the joy flow through them. They reached the yard and saw Gabriel and Katrina looking at the tree line expectantly. They were both confused and in complete shock when 16 wolves came through the tree line.

"Oh my." Katrina breathed recognizing the white wolf.

She and Gabriel linked hands and stepped off the porch. The light gray and black wolves nudged Xavier, Aria, Kiera, and Gage forward. Once they saw the four with them, Katrina and Gabriel realized the wild wolf pack was guarding and guiding them and relief pushed out the initial shock. The four walked slowly through the wild wolves stopping and bowing to the white alpha. The white alpha nibbled on each of their faces as a sign of affection and they went to stand by Gabriel and Katrina.

"Thank you, for our children." Gabriel and Katrina said together and knelt. The white alpha walked to Gabriel and his mate, the black wolf who had taken Xavier, Gage, Aria, and Kiera to safety, approached Katrina. In a human gesture they bowed and placed their muzzles on their shoulders. Gabriel and Katrina stood still in awe of the moment. The snow white alpha male with his night black alpha female turned and trotted out of the yard, their pack following. Within minutes the sounds of paws crunching in the snow faded. The four shifted back and they all went into the house.

"I can't believe it." Gabriel said after listening to the story. "I'm in absolute awe that they rescued you. I can't even get mad right now about the thugs that got by us and were waiting for you, I'm in such awe."

"Dad, have we ever run with the wolf pack before?" Kiera asked.

"The Silver Creek Pack has always respected the real wolf packs in the valley but to my knowledge very few have ever run with them." Gabriel looked at Katrina for confirmation.

"My mother used to run with them." Katrina said, "I guess it just seemed like something my mother did, but no one else did, my mother was always a unique woman."

"I'm not surprised." Kiera grinned and turned to Aria, "Our Grandma Cheri was amazing, she was wild and had a charisma about her that drew both people and other animals in."

"I wish I'd known her." Aria sighed, "I get my mom was trying to protect everyone, but with losing her and my dad it feels like she just took more away from me."

"Aria, I want you to stay here tonight." Gabriel said, "If we can verify, they've left the area after two failed attempts you can stay back at home, but I'm not taking the chance tonight."

Aria nodded at him, "Alright, can I run home for clothes?"

"I'll bring you myself." Gabriel looked at Xavier, "You and Gage go clean up, I'll bring her to get her stuff."

They took three vehicles to school the next morning in case they were ambushed. Aria rode with Xavier. Aria was starting to worry about his silence when he finally spoke.

"We've been getting closer," Xavier said, keeping his eyes on the road. Feeling like an idiot he continued, "Will you be my girlfriend?"

He was going to be an alpha and he was timidly asking Aria to be his girlfriend like some ninth grader. He knew this was the right way to approach it. If she was going to be his mate, he wanted to respect her, and she had never dated before.

Aria was glad he was looking at the road since she was positive her cheeks were turning red. "I kind of thought we were already boyfriend/girlfriend." She said feeling her stomach start to do somersaults.

"I did too but I thought maybe I should ask and make sure you feel the same way." Xavier sighed, relief flowing through him.

"Have you dated before?" Aria asked.

"Yes," Xavier answered her. "Well, I mean I've gone on dates with different girls from school, no pack members though. Since I've always known I would be alpha, I didn't want to show anyone in the pack preference before I was completely sure I wanted to be with them."

"So, you dated regular girls?" Aria clarified.

"Yes. I've been on dates with a few girls including Kelsey. Nothing ever progressed to exclusively dating each other for a long period of time."

"Was Kelsey the most recent one?" Aria guessed,

"Yes but believe me I would never date her again." Xavier was adamant. "She's a nightmare."

"No kidding," Aria agreed.

Chapter 15

They had been driving to and from school together every day for the past two weeks. They had been eating lunch together and Xavier would even drive her home from Katrina's every night just to drive back every morning to pick her up for school. Xavier and Aria were sitting at lunch together as usual, when Aria noticed Kelsey looking at her again. Besides a few snide remarks she hadn't said much about Aria. Even Kelsey realized picking on a girl who lost her father and was now orphaned was not a way to gain sympathy. But now that Aria and Xavier were showing up to school every day together it appeared that Kelsey's jealousy was starting to rear its ugly head again. Kelsey often threw glares at them, but Aria decided she wasn't going to worry about it. But then she had heard in gym class that Kelsey was starting to spread rumors about her. Aria was really upset; she just wanted to be left alone and she was a little bit concerned about the rumors. Some of them were pretty bad. For the most part she knew she would always have close friends in the pack. Recently they had only hung out with a couple of girls at her school who were not a part of the pack. With everything happening with her father, with shifting, and with learning magic it was just safer to hang out with people who wouldn't think she needed to go to the state mental ward if she told them she had spent her evening shifting into a wolf and practicing magic. Aria began to think Kelsey was going to try and hurt her. Aria often wondered why Kelsey wanted Xavier, was it his looks, or the fact he had money, or the few dates they had gone on before Aria had moved to Montana. She couldn't even figure out why Kelsey thought Xavier would want her after how mean she was being.

Xavier was dropping Aria off after school when she finally decided to ask him about Kelsey after focusing on it all day. "I know you have to go to help train, but I have a question for you?"

"Go for it." Xavier said putting the truck in park outside her house.

"Don't get mad, but what did you ever see in Kelsey?" she wondered.

He sighed, trying not to look irritated and not sure how to answer. "I told you before I never wanted to show anyone special treatment in the pack unless I was absolutely sure that I had feelings for them." He sighed, "it's your turn not to get mad, but Aria I am a teenage guy, I dated her cause she was cute."

Aria looked at her shoes, "cute, huh?"

Xavier lifted Aria's face and looked her into her hazel eyes. "Once I got to know her, her cuteness went away, and she was never beautiful to me like you are." He kissed her.

She pulled away, "Don't try and distract me with your kisses." Aria admonished him.

"I need to go," Xavier looked at the clock, he wasn't ready to tell her the depth of his feelings yet. "I can't be late."

"I know I'll see you tomorrow." Aria turned back towards him for a goodbye kiss.

A few hours later Aria was watching YouTube when her phone rang, she saw it was Kiera and answered, "Hello."

"Aria you'll never believe this, but the motion activated cameras picked up Kelsey and some of her friends parking at the bottom of your driveway. They just got out of their car. They're all dressed in black and walking up the rest of the driveway." Kiera explained she was very amused.

"Seriously?" Aria asked in complete shock that Kelsey would be at her house. "What do you think they're going to do?"

"They have a few bags between them." Kiera said, "so I don't know but Greg is here, and he says since it's 9:30 and it's probable that you would be asleep he wants you to turn off the lights quickly and crouch in the kitchen away from any windows."

Aria got up and shut off the TV and the lamp on the end table. "Why do I have to go into the kitchen away from windows?"

Chapter 16

"Dad, Xavier, Greg, Ryan, Gage, and Brian are all on their way there now but before he left Greg told me he wanted you away from the windows because he was worried about them throwing a rock through."

"Oh, okay, I'm in the kitchen sitting on the floor up against the counter. I'll call you when it's over." Aria hung up the phone after Kiera wished her luck. Aria knew something was going to happen. Kelsey had been way too brazen with her harassment last week. She was in complete shock when she heard a window bust. "Are you in there Aria?" Kelsey yelled at the top of her lungs; she was so focused on the house she didn't see her companions' faces go sheer white. "Kelsey, we need to go!" They yelled and ran, dropping their big black bags.

"Where are you two chicken shits going?" Kelsey yelled at their backs. In the silence that followed Kelsey heard the growling. She turned to see six huge dogs growling and snarling at her. She panicked and ran, she fell several times but managed to gain her feet each time and keep going. She looked back and saw the six huge vicious dogs still following her. Her friends were in the car when she got to it, they opened the door and Kelsey jumped in. She started the car and took off.

Aria was standing surveying her broken window. When the six of them got back up to her house. "What am I going to do with this?" She gestured angrily at the window. "It's freezing and I have a huge window gone." Despite her promising herself she would keep it together, tears started to run down her cheeks. Gabriel, Xavier, and Greg shifted, the others turned and disappeared into the forest towards Gabriel's house.

"They'll go get some others and some plywood; we'll get the window covered and, in the morning, call a contractor." Gabriel said as Xavier jumped through the window and wrapped his arms around Aria.

Greg surveyed the damage; "I'm going to take some pictures. While I'm pretty sure we scared the hell out of them, we're going to have you press charges."

Gabriel nodded, "I think that's a good idea. We can't have this type of behavior in our community."

About twelve other pack members arrived in several different pick-ups, with plywood and the tools needed to hang it. They worked together to clean up the glass in Aria's living room and boarded up the large window Kelsey had shattered.

"I took the bags they dropped into evidence," Ryan told Greg. "There were two more large rocks, it looked like each girl carried one, and several cans of spray paint. Had they not been caught they would have caused thousands in damages to Aria's property."

"I took pictures before we started cleaning up. I'll get a statement from Aria tonight. In the morning I'll get Kelsey from school and have her parents meet me at the station." Greg laid out his plan and chuckled, "I bet we scared that little girl straight."

"I bet we did," Ryan agreed.

Two hours later Aria was exhausted. Xavier had started a fire to chase away the chill that had crept through the broken window before it could be repaired. She lay on the couch with Kiera trying to fall asleep. Katrina had tried to convince her to come back home with them, but Aria had insisted on staying home. She was grateful the protection spells and security cameras allowed her to stay in the house. She couldn't keep letting bad things drive her from her home.

She lay there thinking of Xavier who had wrapped his arms around her and kissed her forehead before saying goodnight. He, Greg, Ryan, Gage, and Gabriel had not gotten to their meeting before they had been interrupted by Kelsey. She thought of Kiera who had insisted on staying with her, made her tea like Katrina always did, and let her vent. She thought she would lay there all night but hearing her cousin's breathing start to slow and deepen she slipped into sleep shortly after her.

Xavier, Greg, Ryan, Gage, and Gabriel sat around the table in the guest house Gage and Xavier lived in. "I've been thinking about some of our weaknesses." Greg explained his reasoning for calling the meeting. "We've been really lucky here in Silver Creek Valley. We've always had a pack member as sheriff, we've never really had any problems with neighboring packs with the exception of Tessa's death. We haven't had to worry about DNA or being discovered because we essentially run this town."

Gabriel nodded in agreement, "I know there's enough of us to control and create the outcome we need, and we have enough outsiders that we seem like a normal small town without attracting attention."

"And it's been since my great grandfather's time when we were last attacked by an outside pack," Xavier added, "With the exception of my mother's death."

"Things are changing," Ryan said. "We thought we ran those strange wolves off. We were thinking after all of the attempts they have made in the last week we may need to do more than fight them."

"You mean we may have to kill them?" Gage asked.

"I don't like the idea of this but with DNA and everything we would need to be very careful." Greg warned.

"You're right, we have been largely untested in this department." Gabriel rubbed his forehead. "I don't like this, but I think you're right. We need to start thinking of a more permanent solution to our problem."

Greg nodded, "I have to do some more research, but I wanted to make sure you were on board, and we had your approval."

"I appreciate the respect." Gabriel looked towards the main house. "They will die before they take Kiera."

The others nodded, all nodded in agreement. "They will never touch her," Gage vowed.

"I worry that if we have to kill to protect our territory it will change who we are." Gabriel looked around, "How do you feel about it Xavier?"

"I think that trying to avoid killing should always be our first choice." Xavier wondered if Gabriel was looking for a specific answer. "However, I think that we would be naive not to consider that some enemies will need to be taken out. If this is Tom, he killed my mother, it appears he killed Cassie, he's too dangerous to underestimate."

Gabriel nodded, "I agree." He turned to Greg, "What were you thinking Greg?"

"Well, there's a clearing about 8 miles southeast of Aria's house and about 11 miles southeast of this house," Greg pulled out a map and circled a spot. "This is a defendable area and if someone doesn't make it out, we will not be seen by outsiders."

Gabriel studied the map, "Can we set up a safe zone in a meadow?" he asked, raising his eyebrows in doubt.

"Yes, but not the meadow, if anyone breaches your homes the goal would be to run to this meadow." Greg pointed to the edge of the circle. "This is a cave at the edge of the meadow. I asked Katrina if there was a protection spell you could put on a place. She told me she read it would work with a natural place like a cave but not a manmade house, but it will require blood from those it is supposed to protect."

"Blood?" Xavier asked

"She said it wouldn't take a lot, just a finger prick's worth." Greg clarified.

Gabriel texted Katrina asking her to join them. "Hello, gentlemen." Katrina greeted them as she walked in a few moments later.

Greg smiled at her, "Hello, can you please explain the spell you told me about?"

Gage got up and got Katrina a chair. She sat down and looked at them, "Well as Greg told you, he asked me to see if there was such a thing as a place you could put a protection spell on, like a magic panic room. I remembered coming across a spell like that when Kiera, Aria, Anna and I were researching pack magic. The place has to be all natural like the cave. The spell has to use a bit of blood from every person allowed to cross the protective threshold."

"So, what's the plan?" Gabriel asked, realizing they had worked it all out.

"Katrina, Kiera, Aria, you, Gage, Xavier, Ryan, and I go to the meadow, and we test the protection spell." Greg said.

"How do you test it?" Gabriel asked.

"Aria, Kiera, and I will perform the spell because the three of us are strong individually and even stronger together. We will perform it using blood from everyone but Greg." Katrina started.

"Then I'll try and cross the barrier to 'harm' one of the pack members" Greg explained.

"I think if he just focuses on wanting to hit you" Katrina pointed at Gabriel, "he shouldn't be allowed inside the spell's range which would be the cave."

"If it works, then we take the pack up as a whole, everyone donates a little blood to the spell, and we have a safe place for Aria. All of you here, and the rest of the pack try to make it to the cave in the event of a threat." Greg concluded.

"Alright, I think this is important. We will go tomorrow. Kiera, Aria, Gage, and Gabriel can stay home from school." Gabriel said. "If it works, the whole pack will go up on Saturday."

"We'll be here tomorrow at 8 a.m." Greg said, meaning him and Ryan.

"I'll call Mr. Carr and let him know the kids will not be in school." Katrina said, "We had all better get some sleep."

The next morning, they were all ready to go. They split up in groups, Katrina, Kiera, Greg, and Gage went to the meadow from Katrina's house carrying a chainsaw and clearing a path without it looking too obvious. Gabriel, Xavier, Aria, and Ryan made their way to the meadow from Aria's house clearing a path as they went as well. The paths met about 3 miles from the meadow.

"Alright" Gabriel wiped his forehead with the bottom of his t-shirt. "Chain sawing is a lot of work despite the cold temperatures."

"Agreed." Greg sat in the meadow resting a bit. They all took a few moments to catch their breath.

"Alright everyone but Greg come on over." Katrina got up and started walking to the cave. "Kiera, Aria and I have been practicing."

Kiera handed everyone a finger lancet. "We don't want to interrupt our flow once we start. So, when we say Locul natural ne protejează sângele the third time, all of you lance a finger and squeeze some drops on this side of the entrance." Kiera pointed to the left.

"Then we will move to the middle of the cave and repeat the process, then we will move to the right side and repeat the process." Aria explained.

"So, at each of the three spots lance a finger and squeeze some drops of blood in the same spot we say 'Locul natural ne protejează sângele' for the third time." Katrina clarified. "Three is a powerful number in magic."

"We're going to stand holding hands. We'll say the spell three times in Romanian then three times in English. We will not lance our fingers when we say the English version." Aria told them. "There are also three of us doing the spell, which should make it even more powerful."

"Any questions?" Katrina asked.

Everyone shook their heads no. "Alright let's do this!" Kiera exclaimed.

The three women stood together grasping hands. Gabriel, Gage, Xavier, and Ryan felt the air change. Gabriel was in awe of his mate, she had on a blue coat, blue jeans, and her gray winter hiking boots. Her long red hair flowed around her, Gabriel had never seen her so ethereal. Gage was in awe of Kiera. She was grasping her mother's hand, but she didn't look like a child. Her red hair floated around her purple coat. She looked tall in her black jeans and dark purple winter boots. Her slate gray eyes contrasted with her mother's emerald green ones. Katrina's eyes looked ethereal while Kiera's eyes held mountains that had come to life. Aria stood on the other side of Katrina, Xavier was transfixed by her. She stood with her aunt and cousin but also separated from them somehow. Her strawberry blonde hair was lighter in contrast to their deep red locks; but no less stunning. She had on a dark green coat with black jeans, and black winter boots. She stood majestic like a queen instead of a fiercely primitive warrior like Kiera or an ethereal goddess like Katrina. Everyone watching them in the clearing became mesmerized by them.

Katrina, Aria, and Kiera started together in Romanian, "Protecția locului natural, Loc natural protejează-ți sângele, Locul natural ne protejează sângele, Locul natural ne protejează, Protecția locului natural, Loc natural protejează-ți sângele, Locul natural ne protejează sângele, Locul natural ne protejează, Protecția locului natural, Loc natural protejează-ți sângele," Aria and Kiera lanced their fingers on the hands that were grasp in Katrina's, and Kiera lanced her mother's finger as well. They gently squeezed out some drops. They continued, "Locul natural ne protejează sângele" Ryan, Gage, Gabriel, and Xavier stepped forward lancing their fingers, "Locul natural ne protejează," They finished as the guys finished squeezing out a few drops.

Kiera, Aria, and Katrina switched to English, "Natural place protect, Natural place protect my blood, natural place protect our blood, natural place protect us." They repeated the English three times moving on to the middle then far end of the cave entrance repeating the process again and again.

"Are you alright?" Gabriel asked them concern in his voice as all three fell to the ground after completing the spell.

They all nodded, taking deep breaths. Xavier handed them each a bottle of water from his pack. They let the three of them rest for a while before trying the spell.

"Okay we're ready." Katrina said as they helped each other stand up.

Gabriel nodded and picked up his hand-held radio. "Alright Greg, we are ready."

Greg shifted to his wolf on the other side of the meadow and kept thinking about hurting Gabriel, about biting him. As he ran towards the mouth of the cave where the others stood, he kept thinking of harm. He knew his intent had to be real, so he prepared himself to attempt to bite Gabriel if he was able to breach the barrier. He had to admit to himself that the idea of biting his alpha was difficult to wrap his head around.

Aria's stomach tightened as they all stepped across the cave threshold, she prayed the magic would hold. She needed to believe something could keep them safe from the trespassers who just wouldn't quit coming. She grasped Xavier's hand as Greg grew closer. Greg was in a full out run. Aria squeezed Xavier's hand as Greg reached the threshold. They all jumped when Greg ran headlong into an invisible wall and collapsed.

Everyone stood still a bit stunned it had worked so well, as Greg stood up slowly and shook off the impact. Kiera was holding her breath when Gage rubbed her back reminding her to breathe. As Keira let out her breath, the fog began to lift, and they all jumped with excitement. "It worked!" Katrina shouted, "It really worked!!!"

They were all very excited that the spell had worked, maybe, just maybe, they could put an end to the strange wolf attacks. They all stepped out and checked on Greg. "I'm fine, just a bit stunned," Greg reassured them. "I was hoping it would work but I wasn't expecting thin air to be that solid!"

"This is great, we'll get the whole pack up here Saturday and get the cave to accept everyone." Gabriel said. "Then we find the best way for everyone to evacuate to the cave if there is a need."

"We will also need to keep training how to defend ourselves, whether it be magic or physical." Gage added.

"We'll also need to keep learning how to actually fight." Gabriel looked around, "I don't want to turn our pack into savages, but we cannot afford to be unable to protect ourselves."

"I agree." Greg said.

"Up until the night Tessa was killed our pack had lived in relative peace for a long time." Katrina reached out and grasped Kiera's and Aria's hands, meeting the eyes of everyone in the clearing. "Our pack relished the peace, but we grew soft. Tom and some other wolves killed Tess, they killed my sister, and I'm beginning to fear they killed my parents, Gage's mother, and Xavier's grandparents."

"Katrina?" Gabriel questioned her.

"The timing has been bothering me," Katrina said. "Cassie is killed and within a month five more pack members die in a similar accident?"

"After reading my mom's journals, I agree." Aria squeezed Katrina's hand and looked at Gabriel. "I want to learn to protect myself, to help protect others."

Katrina smiled at the determination in Aria's voice, "We all need to learn, we are done letting them pick us off one by one." Katrina looked at her husband, her mate, her alpha, "They will not lay a hand on my pack, on my son's, on my daughter's." She pulled both Kiera and Aria in, "I may not have given birth to you, but you are mine." she told Aria, kissing the top of her head.

Aria's eyes filled, "You and my mother shared so much. I'm honored you consider me your daughter."

"You are all right, we are done letting them pick us off, they will not harm our pack, our children, we will make this pack strong again." Gabriel turned to Xavier, "Are you up for it?"

"Yes," Xavier drew in a breath, "I will stop him, regardless of who he is."

They spent the rest of the week practicing magic, practicing self-defense, and planning. By Saturday every pack member had a plan. They would all learn the fastest way to the clearing and would practice the route daily. Gabriel had decreed the entire pack would learn to fight. Gabriel, Gage, Xavier, Greg, Brian, Chris, the sheriff's deputies, who were in the pack, set up training sessions. Gabriel made it clear everyone needed to learn. Additionally, Aria, Katrina, and Anna decided to work with every pack member to see who had witch blood. Those who possessed it would practice self-defense spells.

Chapter 17

Friday morning Aria woke up startled to hear someone in her house. She realized that she was surprised, not afraid, so she figured her senses were telling her that she knew the person making noise in her house. She decided to get ready for school before going downstairs. She braided her hair, pulled on a pair of dark blue jeans, a black turtleneck, and a green sweater. She brushed her teeth, washed her face, and pulled on some green wool socks. She looked in the mirror and decided she was ready for the day. She was looking forward to working with Katrina, Anna, and Kiera to protect the whole pack tomorrow. She was excited to watch a movie with Kiera, Gage, and of course Xavier that night. She felt butterflies every time she saw him, and wondered if she would ever get used to him. "Hello?" she called out as she walked down the stairs.

"Hello," a voice she did in fact recognize called back.

"Xavier, did you break into my house?" Aria asked as she reached the bottom of the stairs. The butterflies fluttered in her stomach as she expected.

"I used my key so I'm not sure that is considered breaking and entering." He smiled at her, "plus I made you breakfast."

"Well, I supposed I won't turn you in for breaking and entering since you made me breakfast." She looked at her plate, "Wow, homemade donuts and tea. I'm definitely not calling the sheriff."

"I used a key so at best you could get me for unlawful entry." Xavier tugged her braid, "My grandma loved to cook and taught me how to cook a lot."

"This is so delicious." Aria closed her eyes and took another bite. "You have many hidden talents."

"Well, you are such a good cook I didn't want to let on I knew how, then I might have to take a turn more often." Xavier confessed as he sat next to her and started eating. He thought she was beautiful and strong. He could feel their connection growing and hoped she felt the same. He struggled with his duty to his pack and his duty to her. He wanted to be with her all the time to protect her but knew he had to work with Gabriel to train the pack. He was sure Gabriel felt the need to protect Katrina, just as Gage felt the need to protect Kiera. He knew all wolves both male and female, had a strong drive to protect their mates. He was so caught up in his train of thought it took him a bit to realize he thought of her as his mate. His train of thought was interrupted by Aria's exclamation "Oh this is fantastic. A Chai latte, I love it!"

"You can't tell anyone I cooked for you." Xavier turned to face her. "It will wreck my image."

She laughed, "If you keep taking turns cooking and the food continues to be this good," Aria poked his stomach, "my lips will remain sealed."

He pulled her into him, holding her close and kissing her forehead. "You've got yourself a deal."

She loved the way it felt when he pulled her into him. She felt his strength and felt safe despite all that had happened. She didn't blame the pack for her father's death; she knew that they would have protected him if they had realized he was in danger.

"We better get going." Xavier stood up, "I put the chai in a to go cup so you could finish on the way to school."

Aria and Xavier were at the edge of the parking lot when she realized she had left her water bottle in the truck. "I'll be right back" Aria turned back towards the truck.

"I'll wait here for you." Xavier called after her.

Aria grabbed her water bottle and was making her way back towards the edge of the parking lot where Xavier was waiting for her, when a man got out of a car. "Are you Aria?"

Aria stopped. She didn't sense that the man was a wolf, but she did sense something was off. He was dressed in a disheveled business suit with dark circles under his eyes.

"Who are you?" She asked instead of confirming her identity.

"You need to drop the charges against my daughter." The man said firmly.

"You must be Kelsey's dad." Aria guessed.

"Yes, I'm Mr. Brit, and I don't know what the hell went on at your house that night, but you need to call the sheriff and tell him you want the charges dropped." He reached into his pocket, "I'll write you a check for the damages and this whole ugly business can be over."

"I don't want your money," Aria started to turn away. "I don't think you should be here."

Mr. Brit reached out grabbing Aria's upper arm. "Don't you turn away from me, little lady."

"You're going to want to let go of her." Xavier's voice was low and threatening as he came up behind Aria. His blue eyes went to ice.

Aria pulled her arm from Mr. Brit's grip and stepped towards Xavier.

"This is none of your business, young man, go to class." Mr. Brit said arrogance radiating from him despite his ragged appearance.

"I'm not sure who you think you are, but you need to leave, now." Xavier responded, stepping in front of Aria. He let his alpha presence come out just a bit so the man would know he was not just a mere child. "Your daughter tried to destroy Aria's house, you have no right to come here and try to intimidate her into dropping charges."

"You should be careful son. I know you think that your family is important, but you don't want to bite off more than you can chew." Mr. Brit was enraged that this boy was threatening him, and even more enraged he felt a bit afraid.

"What is going on here?" Mr. Carr asked, approaching the three of them.

"This man was threatening Aria," Xavier turned towards Mr. Carr who immediately saw Xavier's wolf just beneath the surface.

"Mr. Brit, you need to get off school property," Mr. Carr's voice was firm. He was trying to stay calm. "You don't belong here since your daughter's been suspended. You can't harass and intimidate the students."

Mr. Brit turned towards his car, he opened the door looking back at them as he got in. "I don't know what the hell my daughter saw that night, but she is terrified, you are not going to destroy her life over a broken window, this is not over."

"Well great." Aria threw her hands up, "this is just great. We really needed another problem."

"It'll be alright." Xavier tried to soothe her by rubbing her back.

"Don't coddle me." Aria snapped at him and took a step back. "I can't take much more of this."

"Aria, I'll talk to Greg," Mr. Carr tried to reassure her as well, "he will not come near you again." He turned back towards the school, "You two better get to class."

"What is wrong?" Xavier asked irritation in his voice at her response, He was frustrated that she had snapped at him when he had been trying to comfort her.

"I don't need a pat on the back like I'm a two year old." Aria turned towards the building "I'll see you later."

He didn't reach out and grab her arm like he wanted to. Instead, he jogged around her and stood in her way facing her, "why did me comforting you make you mad?"

"Can we talk about this later?" Aria asked, pointing at the school. "I need to get to class."

"Aria" Xavier's voice was full of frustration and barely controlled anger.

"Look I get overwhelmed sometimes, and I just get upset when I think I'm being coddled." Aria walked around him not looking back as she entered the school. She could not figure out why she felt angry when all Xavier was trying to do was help her. She had wanted to lean into him, to let him wrap his arms around her. She wanted to believe it when he told her everything was going to be alright. She also wanted to push him away. Most of the time she felt excited and energized by Xavier and the love she felt for him. Love, that stopped her short and explained why she was scared. She did love Xavier and that terrified her. So far everyone she had loved and counted on for protection, for comfort, had left her. She knew her mom and dad, her grandma Ann didn't leave her by choice, but it still bothered her. She had never even gotten a chance to meet her other grandparents or her grandfather on Joel's side, who had died before she was born. She knew she had Xavier, Katrina, Kiera, Gage, Anna, and the rest of the pack but it was all still new, and it caught her off guard sometimes.

She was on her way to lunch before she knew it, the morning had flown by. She knew she owed Xavier an apology. She had let Kelsey's dad rattle her and she had taken it out on Xavier. She looked around the cafeteria and didn't see him. Her stomach dropped a little, fearing he had decided to skip lunch. She got some food and sat at a table. She was looking down picking at her plate, so she didn't see him approach.

"Am I allowed to sit?" Xavier asked her, his voice was calm but there was a tone in it she recognized as irritation.

"Yes," Aria breathed the word.

He sat his plate on the table, sat down, and looked at her. She could feel his eyes on her. "Alright, I'm sorry." Aria finally met his eyes. "I got mad because I wanted to lean on you and that scares me."

"It scares you?" He raised his dark eyebrows.

"Well, it feels like everyone I get close to dies." Aria huffed out a breath. "I'm ashamed to admit I was scared of Mr. Brit, and I was happy you were there. Then I got mad at myself for being scared and wanting you to make it better. Then I got mad at you because that is better than being mad at myself."

Xavier smiled at her, "I get it, I really do, I have lost a lot too."

Aria tried to hold back tears, but her large hazel eyes let one slip down her cheek. She felt stupid, of course he knew how she felt. Xavier reached across the table and ran his thumb over her pale cheek wiping the tear away. The gesture almost broke her. "Don't cry." Xavier held her hands, "it's alright to get upset and scared, just try not to make me your punching bag."

"I really am sorry." Aria met his blue eyes with her hazel ones so he could see she was sincere.

"Aria I can't guarantee that nothing will happen to me, but I'm strong and I'll do everything in my power to protect you." Xavier whispered, realizing they were beginning to attract some attention. "Let's revisit this later, shall we?"

Aria looked around. "Yes, that's probably a good idea."

After school Xavier was planning on dropping Aria off and going back home to get Kiera and Gage. Gabriel and Greg had texted her that Mr. Brit would be dealt with but when they pulled onto the road that led to the houses a gray truck pulled behind them and began to follow them. Xavier recognized the man in the rearview mirror.

"Aria, please get my cell phone and call Gabriel." Xavier was checking the rear view mirror to make sure Kelsey's dad wasn't going to run them off the road.

"What's wrong?" Aria asked, looking around. Her whole body braced for another attack.

"The infamous Mr. Brit is following us." Xavier slowed down a bit. "Hurry up Aria, call him, so he lowing us. Xavier and I are almost to my house."

"I'll be there, stay in the truck until I get there," Gabriel commanded. "Pass that on to Xavier."

Aria hung the phone up, "he says we have to stay in the truck until he gets here."

Xavier ground his teeth together, "Dammit I wanted to talk to Mr. Brit."

"Xavier." Aria admonished him, "Gabriel said stay put."

They pulled up to Aria's house and Mr. Brit jumped out of his car and headed for Xavier's truck yelling, "You little brat I told you to drop this whole thing. I don't know what the hell is going on up here, but you traumatized my daughter, and she is the one in trouble." He tried the door handle on Aria's side of the truck.

Aria let Xavier pull her into him, this time she did not feel anger at his protection. Aria could tell Gabriel's wolf wanted to meet their attacker head on. They had been under attack so much that Xavier's instincts were in high gear. "Are you okay?" Aria asked him.

"I've never wanted to shift more than I do right now." Xavier gritted between his teeth, his icy blue eyes stared into her hazel ones as every muscle in his body tensed. He tried to focus on the depths of her eyes. "He is trying to attack you, I love you. Every other attack I've been able to fight for you. This time I can't change and fight a normal human."

Aria went still. Xavier had just told her he loved her, and they had a lunatic yelling at them. She stared back into the depths of his blue eyes and could see his wolf. She had never faced his wolf like this before. Xavier's wolf was tense and stiff. He had never wanted to defend someone so much as he did in that moment. Aria could feel her own wolf rise to meet his. She felt more connected to him. As she let her wolf rise Xavier could feel the pull to her increase. He wanted her, he wanted to get rid of the threat outside. He wanted her for his mate. His stomach clenched and he felt the shift start. Aria's connection to him made her stomach clench as well. She was too new to her wolf to understand it meant she was getting ready to shift. Xavier was trying to hold on to his human form when the sound of an approaching vehicle gave him the distraction he needed to reign back in his wolf. He was finally able to close his eyes and break the connection to Aria's wolf. Once the eye contact broke Aria's wolf retreated.

Gabriel's truck pulled into the clearing where Aria's house stood, he got out and walked up to Mr. Brit who didn't even notice him, he was so busy yelling at the truck with Aria and Xavier inside.

"Excuse me," Gabriel said, radiating calm.

"What the hell do you want?" Mr. Brit turned and spat at Gabriel.

"You are on private property attempting to attack a minor." Gabriel pointed out.

"You think you run this town, but I know something is screwed up about you and all your kind." Mr. Brit raised his hands in the air and turned in a circle. "Where the hell are the dogs that chased my girl?"

"Dogs?" Gabriel raised his eyebrows in question.

"Don't play games with me." Mr. Brit took a threatening step toward Gabriel.

"Your daughter came up to this property with the intention of vandalizing and wrecking this home." Gabriel stepped into the threatening gesture, closing the space between them as he gestured to the house. "Your daughter could have hurt someone. You are not in a position to be threatening me or my niece." Gabriel let the wolf come into his dark eyes. The predator glared through them at the man threatening his family.

"I…" Mr. Brit started then trailed off as the hairs rose on his neck and arms. His body was sensing the danger and trying to warn him to back off. He took a step back and tried again, "I'm not finished with you."

Gabriel closed the distance again barely containing his wolf. "You are welcome to take me on anytime, but you are done with Aria. If I see you near her again, you will regret it."

"Are you threatening me?" Mr. Brit barely managed to get the words out. His fight or flight instincts were choosing flight, but he fought the instinct refusing to run.

"No, he meant he would be calling me." Greg said, stepping closer to the pair.

Mr. Brit was shocked. He had been so focused on Gabriel and the threat he posed that he never heard Greg pull up in his Sheriff's car. "It sounded like a threat to me." Mr. Brit turned towards the Sheriff, his fear backing off a bit, now that he thought he was safe with Greg there. But when he met Greg's eyes the fear came rushing back.

Greg too had had enough, and he let his wolf show in his eyes as well. "He will call me and there will be consequences." Greg informed Mr. Brit. "You don't own this town, and we will not tolerate vandalism, harassment, and downright cruelty." It was hard for Greg to step in for his alpha but in the human world Gabriel was not the Sheriff.

"I" Mr. Brit stumbled back towards his car, losing his words. "My lawyer will be in touch." He spat getting into his car and peeling out of the driveway.

"Fantastic" Gabriel quipped.

"Don't worry about him," Greg said "I think he was scared and once he realizes he cannot bully his way out of this he will give up."

"I hope you're right." Xavier walked up to them, Aria by his side.

"I can't believe this." Aria huffed out a breath, putting her hands on her hips. "His daughter nearly gets me eaten by a grizzly bear. His daughter throws a rock through one of my windows and plans to break more. Plus, his daughter had every intention of spray painting my house. And he has the nerve to harass me."

Gabriel smiled at Aria, "He and his daughter are a piece of work, but let's not forget this is partially Xavier's fault."

"My fault?" Xavier protested, "this is not my fault."

Greg started to laugh along with Gabriel as Aria glared at Xavier. "I agree," she growled at him.

"You're the one who decided to take the girl on a date" Greg pointed out. "You need to learn that a pretty face is not the only thing to consider when taking a girl on a date."

"I didn't know she was crazy!" Xavier exclaimed. "I have obviously gotten better as Aria is not only a thousand times prettier, she also has a great personality, and is not crazy."

Gabriel tried to control his laughter, "Good point." He agreed to take sympathy on Xavier.

Aria narrowed her eyes at him, "Are you trying to pull one over on me?

"No, you are everything she is not and more." Xavier looked at Aria with all the sincerity he could muster. He did think she was beautiful, smart, kind, brave, and so much more than Kelsey.

"Well, if he comes back, call me." Greg turned and walked back to his cruiser laughing the whole way.

"Thanks," Gabriel called after him. Greg waved at them and left.

"I agree with Greg. I think that Mr. Brit is done for now but don't take any risks."

"We are already on high alert as it is." Xavier pointed out.

"That's true." Gabriel agreed. "Do you want me to let Gage and Kiera know you are home?"

"Yes, please." Aria reached for Gabriel's hand and squeezed it, "and thank you."

Gabriel gave her hand a gentle squeeze in return and smiled at her. "You did get it right this time." He said to Xavier. "I'll let them know your home." Gabriel walked back to his truck and got in.

"I'm going to grab some wood, I'll meet you inside." Xavier said, starting towards the wood pile.

"Alright" Aria turned and walked towards the house. She decided to go upstairs and change into yoga pants and sweatshirt. When she came back down Xavier was still hauling wood filling all of her wood boxes, so she decided to start making the pizza's they had decided to make for movie night. She had just finished putting the pizza's in the oven when Xavier finished with the wood.

"Those smell good." Xavier sniffed the air.

"They do, and I have a lot since we all eat so much!"

"Aria are we alright?" Xavier asked her, worried she would decide she was angry with him.

"Yes, as much as I wish you had not dated Kelsey, I cannot change your past." Aria walked over to him and put her hands on his shoulder. He was tall but when he was sitting on a stool he was at her height. She let her hands rest on his strong shoulders and let the butterflies dance in her stomach as she touched him. "I wouldn't want to change your past, it has made you who you are. I…" She paused, afraid to speak the words that would change everything.

"What" he asked, pulling her into him so she was standing between his legs.

"You said you loved me in the truck," Aria reminded him.

"I did," Xavier agreed.

I think I love you too." Aria blurted out before she lost her nerve.

He smiled at her, "I know I love you."

She gave him a wry smile, "I guess I know I love you too, it's just," she let out a deep breath, "scary."

He pulled her closer and kissed her. She melted into him, and he deepened the kiss. He ran his hands up and down her back in a soothing momentum. She grasped his shoulders, and the kiss went on. Finally, they pulled apart, "I'm not ready," she said.

"I'm not pushing or even asking," He reassured her. "Let's take things as they come."

She kissed his cheek, "I obviously have better taste than you as I chose you as a first boyfriend and you dated a couple…." She trailed off, not finding the right word.

"Hey," Xavier poked her in the stomach, making her laugh, "At least I got it right this time." He pulled her in for one more kiss, "You do have impeccable taste."

"Xavier?"

"Yes?" He answered her question with a question.

"What happened in the truck?" she needed to know.

"Our wolves were recognizing each other on a whole new level." He explained not sure if she was ready to hear what had really happened. He didn't want to freak her out.

"What level?" she asked the question he was hoping to avoid.

"On a bonded mate level." he answered, his eyes meeting her.

"Bonded mate level?" she questioned as butterflies danced in her stomach.

"My wolf recognizes you as his mate." Xavier purposefully kept his wolf separate from himself to give her time to think.

"I think my wolf recognizes you as her mate as well." Aria whispered quietly looking at the floor. The rush of emotion was overwhelming her. "What does that mean?"

Xavier lifted her chin with one finger drawing her face up to his, his other hand gently swept her golden strawberry hair from her face as he leaned in to gently kiss her lips. "It means that we will become mates one day, but right now we can take it slow."

The timer went off for the pizza, interrupting their conversation. "Saved by the pizza bell." Aria said and was both disappointed and relieved as she went to pull the pizza out of the oven.

They heard their friends pull up outside. "I better make sure that it's actually Gage and Kiera." Xavier stood and walked to the front of the house. "It's them," he called to her.

"Good, I'm starving." Aria called back.

They watched a couple movies, ate pizza, and relaxed for the first time in a while. All of them knew this may be one of the last peaceful nights they had in a while. They also feared the night wouldn't stay peaceful. Between the intruders making attempt after attempt to abduct Kiera, and Kelsey and her dad harassing Aria, they felt as though things would never calm down.

"Do you think Tom is behind all of this?" Kiera asked them when the credits started to roll on the movie.

"At first, I wasn't sure," Aria looked at Xavier gauging his reaction, "but now that I have read more of my mom's journals, I think it is."

"I think it's him as well." Xavier didn't want the others to be afraid to discuss things around him.

"Are you alright with this?" Aria asked Xavier.

"Yes, for the most part I don't think about him as my dad." Xavier looked at each of them so they could see the sincerity in his eyes.

"I heard my mom and dad talking," Kiera looked at her hands, "they think Tom killed Grandma Cheri, Grandpa Richard, Natasha, Fred, and Emma."

Xavier looked at her, "Really?"

"Please don't say anything. I know they were just throwing around ideas, dad will tell you if they find any real proof." Kiera pleaded, "I shouldn't have said anything."

There was a pause, "I was thinking the same thing." Gage, Xavier, and Aria said in unison.

They all grinned at each other and the tension in the room dissipated. "It's alright, I've thought about Tom a lot. I've talked it over with Gabriel, and before my grandparents died, I'd talk to my Grandpa Fred. They both told me that it came down to choice." He sighed, "that my blood doesn't determine who I'm."

"They are right." Gage agreed. "But I know you don't always believe that. Think of me, my dad is some loser loner wolf who ended up abusing my mom."

"I know, and I don't think you are a loser but I'm working on believing the same about myself." Xavier rubbed his forehead. "But you're right, I don't judge others based on who their parents are, why am I doing it to myself?"

"We better get some sleep." Gage tapped his watch, "It is getting late. Are you guys ready?"

"I'm going to stay here." Xavier told Gage and Kiera. "On the couch," he pointed out when Kiera grinned at Aria.

Gage poked Kiera, "knock it off."

"What?" Kiera asked innocently. "Can't I look at my cousin?"

Gage rolled his eyes and grabbed Kiera's hand dragging her towards the front door. "See you in the morning."

Aria and Xavier bid them good night as they walked out the front door.

"There are more blankets in the ottoman if you need them." Aria told Xavier.

"I'll be fine, your couch is comfy. See you in the morning," Xavier kissed Aria's forehead, "sweet dreams."

She smiled at this new habit of his, she stood on her tiptoes to pull him down for a kiss on the lips, "good night." she said with a satisfied grin as he gasped for breath from the surprise of her forcefulness.

Xavier was up and had breakfast on the table before Aria made it downstairs the next morning. She was touched when she saw he had included all her favorites, even her an iced chai latte.

Chapter 18

They made it to Katrina's and Gabriel's bright and early the next morning. Xavier had the entire pack would be arriving soon. Aria, Kiera, Katrina, and Anna were gathering supplies. They had decided to light candles and had some herbs and essential oils that, according to some texts, strengthened magic. Gabriel, Xavier, and Gage were discussing the following week's training schedule. Greg and his deputies arrived first, but soon after the pack started trickling in and before long everyone was present.

Gabriel stood and cleared his throat. The whole pack went silent. "We are going to a clearing up in the mountains." He explained. "There is a cave up there that will be our safe spot in case the intruders come back looking for a fight. We will all need to prick our fingers and give a tiny amount of blood. If any of you are concerned about your little ones donating a little blood via finger prick, come talk to Katrina or me. After we complete the ritual, we will work with all of you individually or in family units so that you all know the fastest way to get to the cave. Additionally, we have set up training times for everyone to learn self-defense. You will all need to sign up for two training times. One to learn self-defense and fighting skills and one training time to learn about magics. We will go from there. You will find out if you can do magic with Katrina." He looked around, taking in the pack's mood. He sensed some were excited, some were scared, but most were determined. "This is our territory. We will protect it." He paused, letting the wolf's territorial drive rise to the surface and feeling his pack's answer drive. He took a deep breath of the crisp air and continued, "We have been largely unchallenged for decades. We have been privileged to have enjoyed peace. But in the last two decades we have enjoyed a false sense of peace by ignoring an enemy. That enemy has been picking us off one by one over the years. That enemy is knocking on our door again, ignoring the threat did not make it disappear. We will not long ignore this threat any longer. We will learn to fight, we will be strong, and we will defend our territory."

Voices of agreement rose up across the pack and Gabriel knew he had said the right thing. He looked to Xavier who was standing by his side. "We will work together and take our peace back." Xavier broadcasted his voice over the pack, "We will not get complacent again. When this enemy is defeated, we will remain watchful."

The pack's assent grew louder. Gabriel gave them all a moment to express their unity, "Let's go, anyone with questions, feel free to ask." Gabriel concluded.

The pack all started towards the clearing. Everyone would sign up for training after the protection spell was in place. They made it to the clearing and started organizing everyone. They handed out finger lancet's to everyone. Four pack members had driven all over the nearby city to get enough for the pack to use for the spell.

"We will be speaking in Romanian." Katrina told the pack members, "We don't want to interrupt our flow once we start." Katrina explained as she had before when it was just a few of them in the clearing. "When we say Locul natural ne protejează sângele the third time, all of you lance a finger and squeeze some drops on this side of the entrance." She pointed to the left. "Then we will move to the middle of the cave and repeat the process, then we will move to the right side and repeat the process. At each of the three spots squeeze some drops of blood in the same spot we do." Katrina grasped Kiera and Aria's hand. "Kiera, Aria and I are going to stand holding hands. We will say the spell three times in Romanian then three times in English. We will not lance our fingers when we say the English version." Katrina looked at everyone. "Any questions?"

No one spoke up so Katrina, Kiera, and Aria moved to the first side of the entrance of the cave and as they had before started the spell together in Romanian, "Protecţia locului natural, Loc natural protejează-mi sângele, Locul natural ne protejează sângele, Locul natural ne protejează, Protecţia locului natural, Loc natural protejează-mi sângele, Locul natural ne protejează sângele, Locul natural ne protejează, Protecţia locului natural, Loc natural protejează-mi sângele," Aria and Kiera lanced their fingers on the hands that were grasp in Katrina's, and Kiera lanced her mother's finger as before so they did not have to let go of each other. They gently squeezed out some drops. They continued slowly giving the pack time to come up, "Locul natural ne protejează sângele." Each pack member stepped forward lancing their fingers. They waited until the last pack member squeezed out a few drops, "Locul natural ne protejează," they finished.

Kiera, Aria, and Katrina switched to English, "Natural place protect, Natural place protect my blood, natural place protect our blood, natural place protect us." They repeated the English three times moving on to the middle and the other end of the entrance of the cave repeating the process again and again this time with the entire pack.

"It doesn't look different," Cory commented once the spell was complete and Kiera, Aria, and Katrina were resting on the lawn chairs that had been brought for them.

"It doesn't but we tried it, it works." Gabriel told him, raising his voice so other pack members could hear. Cory nodded, trusting his alpha and moved on.

They all lingered in the meadow going in and out of the cave. The younger pack members were throwing snowballs at each other. It was a warm day despite the lingering snow. They all played for a bit, some of them shifting into wolf and bear form wrestling around the meadow. After a few hours they all started back towards Gabriel and Katrina's house.

"I'm sorry for everything that has happened." Kiera said to Aria walking alongside her. "So don't take this the wrong way when I say, I am so glad you came here."

Aria took her cousin's hand, "I know what you mean."

"I love Anna," Kiera looked around, "but we have a connection I can't explain. I am sorry coming here meant losing your dad as well."

"If Tom is behind all of this it's likely he would have found my dad and me at some point." Aria took a deep breath. "I grew up an only child and now I have a sister."

Kiera leaned into Aria, "Ahh, I agree."

They walked hand in hand leaning into each other. Magic flowed between them. They strengthened each other. Katrina could sense the magic flowing and smiled. She missed her sister, but she found joy in her sister's child, and she would take her sister's place and care for Aria. She would help Aria grow into a strong, brave, independent woman. She would do that for her sister, and she would do that for Aria. Katrina was scared that she would lose one of them to the enemy they faced. She knew Tom was behind these attacks, she knew he was responsible for her sister's death, and now she was beginning to fear he had killed her parents, Xavier's grandparent, and Gage's mother. Gabriel had been right when he told the pack they had had false peace over the last decade and a half. The pack had had an enemy in Tom since the night he met Tessa. He had been picking them off one by one and they had let him. She feared now he would take one of the most precious things in her life, Kiera. She feared he would go for Aria or Xavier as well. She would continue to go through her mother's and their ancestor's journals. She would continue to face her fear of magic. She would get stronger. She would learn what she needed to learn and more. She would stand with Gabriel and protect her children and her pack. She would teach them to protect themselves and their pack.

"Are you alright?" Gabriel asked as he walked up next to her.

"I'm fine, why?" Katrina asked, thinking the man could read her mind.

"Well," he gave her an odd look, "Your hair is floating, and it is not that windy."

"Oh." Katrina lifted her hand to feel her hair, "Well I was thinking of protecting our children and our pack. It seems the more we practice magic the more it shows" She patted her hair.

"We will." Gabriel wrapped his arm around her, "we will protect all of them."

"Not fast enough," Xavier admonished Aria.

"I can't go any faster," she complained, "I'm not a track star." She collapsed on the ground. She felt hot despite the fact she lay on the snow.

"Come on Dora, get your butt up." Kiera stood over Aria grinning as she spoke.

Aria glared at her, "You're lucky I don't have the energy to get up right now."

"I know it is the third time we have made this run today," Xavier conceded. "But we all agreed we would practice four times today."

Aria turned her glare on Xavier, "Yesterday we performed a powerful protection spell with the entire pack, tomorrow is Monday, and we are back to school. We have plans to practice this route everyday AND practice magic AND practice self-defense!" Aria exaggerated the word 'and' every time as she listed her list. "AND I'm tired. AND I'm done for today." She was starting to shiver as her body cooled and the wet, cold ground began to soak into her.

"You need to shift, or you're going to get sick." Xavier told her, his tone low and irritated.

"Come on, Xavier." Gage cajoled him, "she is trying."

Aria rolled onto her stomach, taking a deep breath letting her nose fill with the earthy scents all around her. She thought of cozy bear dens and snuggly baby bears. She knew she was romanticizing a bear's den, but it worked, soon she felt her body change to bear.

"Wow!" Kiera was shocked. Aria had not changed to her bear form since the first day they had all tried.

Aria took a moment to adjust to her new size and weight. She slowly stood on all fours getting her balance. Once she had her balance she reared up on her hind legs and roared at Xavier. Her roar was loud and fierce. When she finished, she turned and headed back towards her house.

"Well, she told you!" Gage laughed.

Xavier rolled his eyes as Kiera and Gage shifted to their bear forms as well and followed Aria. He knew he was pushing her hard. He knew she was tired and had already run to the cave a couple times today. He should have been more gentle about pushing her, but he was so afraid she would be hurt, he wanted to make sure she could get to safety. He sighed, he owed her an apology. He shifted to his wolf and ran back to his house.

Aria got to her house and shifted back to human. She turned to see Gage and Kiera coming up behind her. They shifted as well and looked around. "We thought Xavier was right behind us." Gage said, looking around again.

"I don't care if he comes, I need a break." Aria grumbled walking into the house.

"He is only pushing you cause he is scared someone will hurt you." Gage told her back.

"Aria, you know he wasn't trying to be a jerk." Kiera added.

Aria huffed out a breath, "I know, look I love you guys, and I appreciate the practice, but I'm going to take a shower and relax."

"We love you too," Kiera responded. Then keeping her voice chipper she smiled and added "see you tomorrow for practice."

Aria turned in the doorway, "Oh joy, see you then," she quipped.

Aria walked in her house and shut the door behind her. She knew Xavier cared and she had promised him she would not use him as a punching bag but dang if he didn't make her mad. She didn't think it was her fault this time. He just kept pushing her, she was exhausted. She climbed up stairs to her bedroom and undressed while she ran herself a warm bath. She added some lavender bath bombs she had gotten while shopping with Katrina and Kiera. She decided to go all out and lit some vanilla scented candles. She sank into the warm purple water and felt it begin to relax her tense muscles. Once the water started to sooth her body she began to second guess snapping at Xavier. Maybe she had been too hard on him. She was a bit worried he hadn't gone back to her house. She didn't know if he was still out in the woods or if he had gone back to his house instead. She knew he had two training sessions that afternoon, and wondered if he would call her. It was Sunday, she wanted to relax and snuggle up on the couch with Xavier not run as fast as she could through the woods. She thought back to Philadelphia. On Sunday's her and Grandma Ann would make elaborate meals. They would make a big breakfast and a big dinner. They would go all out and set the table with fancy place settings, despite the fact it was usually just the two of them. She remembered how much fun they had and all of the recipes that she had learned from Grandma Ann. Spending so much time in the comfort of the old Victorian in Philadelphia had helped her heart heal as she grieved her mother's loss. It occurred to her that she had not had that comfort and warmth to grieve her father's loss. Sure Katrina,

Gabriel, Gage, Kiera, and Xavier had all been there for her along with Brian, Chris, and the rest of the pack, but there had also been fear, fighting, and constant turmoil. She had no time to heal. She thought now that was what was contributing to her outbursts and that was why she had been hard on Xavier this afternoon.

She couldn't help but smile a bit as she lay there thinking it through. Everyone had been shocked when she had shifted to her bear form rather than her wolf form. Xavier had hid it well but she could see she had surprised him by roaring at him. Her smile faded as she remembered the look on his face before she had turned and went home. Had she seen sadness? She could have held on to her righteous feeling of irritation if she had seen anger or pride in his eyes but the glimpse of sadness she saw had the anxiety she had gone too far rising up in her again. She lay in the bath until it cooled. When she realized she was full of goosebumps she got out. She put on red yoga pants and a black sweatshirt. She braided her hair and pulled on thick black wool socks. The house was a bit chilly, but she didn't have the energy to start a fire. She went downstairs and curled up on the couch with a blanket. She was going to grab a book, but the house really was cool. She told herself she would get up, grab a book, and check the thermostat as soon as she warmed up a bit. She fell asleep instead.

Xavier was already home when Kiera and Gage ran into the yard. They had run home as wolves and wrestled a bit before shifting back to humans.

"How is she?" Xavier asked them.

"She's just tired." Kiera poked him in the chest, "Can't you give her a break?"

Xavier rubbed the spot Kiera poked, she had not been gentle, and he had felt it through the jacket he had pulled on to keep the cold at bay. "I know, I'm just scared she'll be alone when they come for her again."

Xavier's words stopped Kiera's irritation, "We all want her safe." Kiera said, "but we need to remember she is still getting used to everything."

"Kiera they are after you as well, I understand how Xavier feels" Gage huffed out a breath, "It is terrifying to think we may not be strong enough to stop them.

Xavier reached out, putting his hand on Gage's shoulder in comfort. "I worry about Kiera as well." Xavier reached out with his other hand and grasped Kiera's hand. "We will be strong enough," he squeezed Gage's shoulder, "plus this one has no quit in her." He pulled Kiera in for a hug.

"Neither does Aria, she just needs to recuperate a bit, she will be back at it tomorrow." Kiera defended Aria.

"I know" Xavier reassured her, "I wasn't putting her down. I'll go see her after training and work things out."

By the end of the training sessions Xavier had a plan all worked out for mending things with Aria. He showered and headed into town. He stopped and picked up food, dessert, flowers, and a gift. He thought he would cover all his bases and figured she had been too tired to make herself food. He pulled up to the front of her house just past dark. It worried him a bit to see all of the lights off, but then he thought she must have fallen asleep. He carried all of his bags to the porch and let himself in. He was surprised how cold it was inside the house.

"Aria," he called out.

She woke at the sound of her name, "Hello, Xavier?" it came out as a question.

He walked around the big stone fireplace, "There you are sleepy head. I've brought food."

"Really?" she was surprised, "I thought you would be mad at me."

"I was at first, but then I realized I was being a jerk." Xavier sighed and grinned at her, "I know I'm surprised as well, it's so rare I'm in the wrong.

"Very funny," she rolled her eyes at him.

"Aria, it's really cold in here." Xavier walked over to the thermostat.

"I know it's how I fell asleep." She explained, "I was going to get up, grab a book, and check it. But while I was waiting to warm up a bit, I passed out from exhaustion."

"It's only 50 degrees here." Xavier walked over to the stove and turned a knob. The stove made a click, click, click sound but no flame ignited. "You're out of propane."

"What?" Aria could feel her face turning red. "Oh man, Gabriel offered to check for me and I insisted he let me check." She groaned, "with everything going on I completely forgot."

"Let's go out and check the tanks to confirm." Xavier grabbed a flashlight off the shelf, and they walked to the entryway to put on boots and coats.

Xavier lifted the lid on the propane tank and shined his flashlight on the gauge.

"Crap, it's completely empty." Aria smacked her forehead, "I'm such an idiot."

"I'll start a fire; you should call Gabriel and see if he's ever had the propane company come out after hours." Xavier started to the woodshed to grab some kindling as Aria trudged inside to call Gabriel.

"What did he say?" Xavier asked, slipping off his boots and carrying the kindling over to the fireplace.

"He said they will charge me extra, but they will come. We are supposed to get some freezing rain tonight in the early morning hours, so he suggested I call and pay the fee."

"Did you get an 'I told you so' from him?" Xavier asked.

"No, he was super nice about it." Aria sounded relieved. "He said we have all been under an enormous amount of stress and he had better go check the tanks at your guy's houses as well."

Xavier smiled at her, "He has a soft spot for you." Xavier lit a match and the large fireplace soon erupted in flames. "We will be warm soon; I'll go start the fireplaces in each of the other rooms while you call. When you're done do you want to dish up the food? I even have dessert."

"Thank you," was all Aria could think to say. She was very grateful he was there but didn't know how to express it without sounding foolish.

They ate and talked while they waited for the propane truck to arrive. Aria opened her present and felt a bit bad for snapping at him. "I'm really sorry I snapped at you." She said again as she took out a pretty floral journal with a matching pen, a candle, and a box of her favorite chai tea.

"I was being pushy," Xavier conceded. "I meant it when I said there was no need for you to be sorry earlier."

They sat and watched TV as the fires warmed the house. Xavier got up every so often to add wood to each of the fires. The house was already up to 70 degrees by the time the propane truck arrived a while later. The man filled their tank, checked for leaks, and relite Aria's furnace and hot water heater. He told her the stove and dryer would automatically light when she used them next. She was grateful her dad had gone through what ran on propane with her in case there was a problem while he was on the road. Of Course, Joel didn't know at the time he would be gone forever, and Aria would need to know all the time.

They went back to finish their movie after the man left. Xavier could feel Aria's body relax into sleep within minutes. He wanted to stay with her all night, but they had agreed to take things slow. They were young and there was so much going on right now he didn't want to take things in a direction she may not be ready for. He was going to be Alpha one day, so he had to be careful. He finished the movie with her sleeping by his side. He carried her up to her bed, laying her down and covering her up. He bent over and kissed her forehead. He thought she was beautiful and couldn't believe he was lucky enough to have her. He hoped he would be able to keep her. He hoped they would all be ready when the enemy came again. He left her a note on the counter, locked up, and went home. He checked the security cameras before he went to bed to reassure himself, they were working.

They practiced all week getting to the safe spot. They would practice running there from Aria's house, from Kiera's house. She practiced with everyone. She was now able to make the trip in what Gabriel and Xavier called an acceptable time.

Chapter 19

Aria woke up looking forward to the day. The entire pack including Aria had been practicing every day for two weeks straight. They practiced running to safety, they practiced witch magic, and they practiced combat fighting. She swore every cell in her body ached. But today would be different. Gabriel had decreed the entire pack would rest this weekend. He had told them all that he was proud of how hard they had been working and the progress they had made.

Aria took her time getting up. She had the first part of the day to herself, then she and Kiera were going to make Gage and Xavier dinner, play board games, and watch a movie. Aria took a bath, then made herself breakfast. After breakfast she curled up on the couch and read. She had just finished her book when she heard a vehicle pull up. Startled, she sat up and looked at her phone. It was already 2pm, she had become completely lost in her book. She got up to let Kiera in.

"Ready to cook?" Kiera asked as Aria opened the door.

"Let's do this!" Aria answered, smiling at her cousin and taking one of the bags she held.

"I have everything we need to make stuffed shells, garlic bread, and tiramisu." Kiera set her bag down. "I even grabbed a bottle of nonalcoholic wine so we could feel fancy."

They pulled out all of the food and started to cook. "Gage kissed me." Kiera blurted out as Aria was filling the large pasta shells with cheese.

"When?" Aria asked, setting down the shell and picking up the next.

"Last night." Kiera sighed. "We're always really careful, we don't want to make my dad mad."

"Do you think he will kiss you again?" Aria wondered.

"I do," Kiera hesitated, "but I think it'll be a while. With us living so close I think it will freak my parents out if we get too close too fast. I mean we've been friends since we were babies, but about a year ago things started to change."

"I think slow is good, but it's hard." Aria admitted.

"Hard for you too." Kiera asked.

"Yes, Xavier and I are going to take our time." Aria smiled, "but we kiss a lot."

"Don't rub it in." Kiera threw a spoonful of the cream she was topping the tiramisu with at Aria.

"I wasn't," Aria exclaimed indignantly.

Kiera started laughing and threw another spoonful at her, "Yes you were."

"We sit on the couch and kiss for hours and it is amazing." Aria managed to get out between bouts of laughter. When Kiera threw a third spoonful of cream at her, Aria flung a spoonful of spaghetti sauce back at her.

The two of them were wrestling on the kitchen floor covered with food when Xavier and Gage walked in. "Should we order take out?" Gage asked, looking down at them.

"I think we should hose them off." Xavier chimed in.

"Don't you dare." Gage warned Kiera seeing the gleam come into her eyes.

"What?" Kiera asked innocently.

"You know what." Gage reached down and picked Kiera up before she could throw food at him. "I'm throwing this one in the shower before she throws food at me." Gage walked Kiera into the downstairs bathroom and put her in the shower fully dressed. Kiera was laughing too hard to say anything.

"We have enough for dinner." Aria told Gage and Xavier as Gage walked back in.

"Will you throw the baking dish with the stuffed shells in the oven? I'm going to take a shower. I'll be back down with clothes for Kiera, and we will clean up the floor." Aria smiled at the guys and walked to the stairs her head held high like a queen.

When the girls were finished showering and dressing, they were surprised to find the guys had cleaned the kitchen. "What a great surprise!" Aria exclaimed.

"Well, you two cooked, we cleaned," Xavier said.

"Next time maybe don't get food everywhere." Gage suggested.

They had a nice evening. As planned, they ate, played games, and watched movies. They all felt like it had been a well needed break. They all said goodnight as the evening ended. Gage and Xavier were going with Gabriel and Greg in the morning to meet with Cory and Sarah, the alpha pair from the Coeur d'Alene pack. Due to the early morning, Xavier decided not to stay at Aria's house. Kiera was going with Anna for breakfast. Aria had told Kiera she should have some one on one time with Anna so she didn't feel replaced. Gage and Kiera left in Kiera's car as Xavier lingered to say good night again.

"Goodnight." Xavier leaned down and kissed Aria.

"Goodnight." She said as his lips parted from hers.

She watched him walk to his truck wishing she didn't have to be so damn responsible. She waved at him as he drove off. She locked up her house and went upstairs to bed. She was feeling relaxed for the first time in a long time. She lay there thinking of Xavier as she drifted off to sleep.

She woke to the sound of someone breaking a downstairs window. She immediately knew she was in real danger, her senses were screaming at her to run. She had to go out her patio door and off the balcony to the woods. She knew where to go; she just had to get there. She quietly opened her patio door, the frigid night air and the fear raising the little hairs on her arms. She was wearing dark purple cotton pajama pants and a matching cotton t-shirt; she was not dressed for the cold, so she shifted to wolf mid-leap, her front paws quietly crunching on a patch of snow, her back paws landing on brown grass. She knew they heard her impact with the ground, but she didn't look back. She ran through the woods on four legs, her body sensing someone behind her as it began to snow. Gabriel had told her to run, run as fast as she could to the spot. Xavier and she had practiced, Kiera and her had practiced, she was just supposed to run. She pictured Xavier kissing her for the first time on Valentine's Day. She pictured the last evening she had spent with her dad, watching TV and eating popcorn. She pictured Katrina making her a cup of tea when she had a bad day. She pictured Kiera sitting across from her as they talked into the night. She pictured Gabriel kneeling before her apologizing for not protecting Joel. She felt the love and anger simultaneously rise in her. She risked a glance behind her and saw two wolves were gaining on her. She felt the love and anger begin to push out the fear despite realizing she would not make it to the protected cave. With this thought came the realization that her mother was in her, Katrina was in her, her strong, magical ancestors' blood was coursing through her body. Her Father's love was in her, her Grandma Ann's kindness was in her. She realized she had everything she needed to turn and fight, but she could not take on the two pursuing wolves as a wolf. She needed to turn back to human and draw on the magic, the love, the strength, and the perseverance of her ancestors. If she could set a protection perimeter her pack would find her and help her. She believed it with every fiber of her being. They were pack and they would come for her. Completely blocking out fear and letting her instincts rise in her, she changed back to human as she turned, throwing her hands up and shouting "proteja pe mine".

They could feel her fear. It woke them. Xavier and Gage raced to the main house. They were met by Katrina, Gabriel, Brian, Kiera, and Chris. "There's no time to wait for help, the others will come when they can, I sent the alert."

"Kiera?" Chris asked as they ran towards the woods.

"She has to come, we cannot afford to split up." It was the last thing Gabriel managed to say before shifting. As practiced Xavier, Gabriel, and Chris shifted to their wolf form while Brian and Gage shifted to their brown bear form. By now the whole pack had been alerted and would come, but they could all feel they would be too late. The enemy in the woods would be defeated, or victorious, before the others made it. They were strong and Gabriel had to believe they would vanquish this enemy tonight on their territory.

They ran as though they were the wind. They made it to the spot as the light snow began to pick up, but they didn't see Aria. Kiera and Katrina shifted back to human. "She hasn't been here, she never made it." Katrina gasped. She was scared but she could feel that something had changed. Aria was not as afraid as she had been. It had been her fear running through the family and pack bond that had woken them.

"I can feel she's close." Kiera told them.

Gabriel turned back towards the woods and following instinct took off running to where he could feel her. Katrina and Kiera shifted, and they all followed him. As they ran Xavier was sending his thoughts towards Aria. He had no idea if it would work but he had to focus on something constructive as he ran because the thought of losing her was too much to bear.

The wolves who had killed Aria's father were surprised when the little she wolf abruptly stopped, turned back to human, and yelled something at them. The two were even more surprised when they ran headlong into an invisible wall. Aria held her hands out strong and steady now. She felt her pack was on the way, she hoped it was really happening and was not just wishful thinking. When the two wolves had run into her shield, it had almost knocked her over, but she had stayed steady. They didn't seem to notice how much strength it took to maintain the shield, something she was very grateful for. If they knew that beating at the shield would weaken her, they would try and get her to drop it.

Two more wolves came out of the woods joining the first two. "Good you got her," one said once he'd shifted to human.

Aria stared, she could not believe her eyes. She had only seen a picture of him when he was a teenager, but she knew this was Tom, Xavier's biological father. His dark eyes looked soulless, his face was sun weathered, and he stood around 6 feet tall. Her blood ran cold, this man was the reason her mother had left her. This man was the reason her father was dead. This man was the reason Xavier didn't have a family. She almost lost her concentration and dropped the shield, but she knew if she dropped the shield, they would have her.

"Aren't you the spitting image of your mother?" Tom started to pace along the barrier. "She was always a strong witch wolf." He paused and scanned Aria and the surrounding woods. "But she wasn't so strong the night I killed her."

Aria's face didn't change. Tom didn't know that Cassie had sent Katrina a letter telling her she feared Tom had located her and she feared for their safety. Aria knew Tom was trying to manipulate her into dropping her shield. "Interesting, you're not surprised to see me. I left you and your father alive because I was hoping to see if you were a wolf. But you had already hit puberty, and nothing happened. Then my man trailing you lost you and your father when you moved." Tom was surprised the teenager before him was not wavering. "I saw you and my boy in the city a few weeks ago. He likes you; I can tell. I'm not going to hurt you, Aria. I just want you to come with me. I can teach you to be strong and you can still be with Xavier. My son will join my pack, and we will be strong. He can keep you as his mate if you come with me now."

"Xavier will never leave our pack for yours." Aria told Tom. Her belief in the truth of her words strengthened her shield.

"You know Joel was not your father, right?" Tom smiled when he saw the confusion begin across Aria's face. "After your mother's spell almost killed us all. We had to leave. Your mother left the next morning. Evan found her and he finally convinced her he had not betrayed them. They began their relationship living in an apartment in Portland months after Tessa's death. Evan tried to start reigning your mother in and they ended up getting into a huge fight. Evan lost his temper and struck Cassie. She lost it right back and the two of them fought. Evan left after hurting your mother. He called me and said he didn't know what to do. He loved her, but she needed to start being a more submissive mate. I tried to explain to him she had alpha and beta blood coursing through her veins and reining her in would be difficult. I told him I would come help take her to a new location where we could work on bringing her around together."

"Sir" one of the other wolves interrupted him.

Tom turned towards a teenage boy who had shifted from his wolf form, interrupting them. "What?" His voice barely controlled anger.

"I can hear others coming." the boy stuttered out.

"Kendra has cast a spell that will confuse them as to her location." Tom looked at Aria as he spoke and not at the young boy who had delivered the warning.

"Sorry for interrupting sir" The boy said, sensing that he had crossed a line. He knew Tom was not to be interrupted, but now he knew why he had brought Kendra with them.

Aria wasn't sure if he was lying to scare her or if her pack really wasn't going to be able to find her. She knew Tom was an experienced manipulator. She had to hold strong to her belief that her pack would find her. She didn't let her facial expression change at his words.

Tom studied her, "As I was saying, Evan stayed away for a bit hoping Cassie would calm down and he could speak with her." Tom continued. "When Evan and I returned to the house several hours later Cassie was gone. Cassie likely left shortly after Evan and never returned." Tom sighed, "he shouldn't have left. He didn't know a whole lot about keeping his women in line at that time. We searched the city, but Cassie was truly gone this time. Evan decided to move with me. When we were cleaning out the apartment, we found a pregnancy test in the trash in the bathroom. Your mother was pregnant with you when she left that apartment in Portland and that makes Evan your father."

"She may have lost that baby." Aria couldn't help but respond. She loved Joel and didn't want to think he wasn't her father. She realized that in their hurry to learn as much magic as possible she had not been able to read every word of her mother's diaries. What she had read started to come to her in a different light. She knew Tom was right now putting her mother's written words together with what Tom was telling her.

"Ah but remember three years ago we caught up with your mother. We were finally able to trace her." When we caught up with her in New York State it was about 14 years and 2 months after the day she left the apartment in Portland." Tom paused to let that sink in. "I believe you were 13 years and 3 months old when your mother met with an unfortunate," He stopped the sentence early to let his words sink in.

Aria could feel the tears involuntarily beginning to fall. "Why should I believe you?" She regretted the words the second they were out, she was letting Tom get to her, she had to keep her composure.

Tom smiled at the young women in front of him. She was in her pajamas, but she held herself so regal she could have been a queen in a gown. The tears running down her face did not detract from her regal beauty, it only made her more stunning. Her beauty angered him. He tried to calm himself, he could not harm her if he wanted his son to come with him. He thought he was getting into her head and knew that if he could distract her enough her shield would fall. Then he would have her and a way to get his son.

Gabriel, Katrina, and Xavier realized they had been running in a wide path around the place that they could feel Aria without ever getting closer to her. They stopped. Xavier, Gabriel, Katrina, and Kiera shifted back to human, Gage, Brian, and Chris stayed in animal form on high alert to protect their vulnerable pack members from a surprise attack.

"Something isn't right." Xavier growled.

"Calm down, take a breath." Gabriel was talking to Xavier and himself.

"I think it is Tom." Katrina blurted out unsure of how to ease into it with such little time. Gabriel, Xavier, and Kiera stared at her, and Gage moved closer to Kiera. "There is a feel in the air. I think there is a spell being used to prevent us from going directly to Aria. The air feels electric and sinister at the same time. I remember the feel from the night, the feel from Tessa's body. I know this is hard, but Tom will try to manipulate you, Xavier. We need to get to Aria."

"Do you know how to break the spell?" Gabriel asked Katrina.

"Unfortunately, I don't." Katrina responded. "But I think there is a work around."

"Yes," Kiera responded.

Katrina nodded at her and turned to Xavier. "I know this will be hard, but I think you are the only one who can find Aria. Tom is your biological father, you share blood. I think if you focus on that you can lead us to him, which will lead us to Aria,"

"Why can't you focus on Aria, she is your niece?" Xavier asked.

"I think they would've thought of that, the only way to break a blocking spell according to the texts I've read is by a direct blood tie. I think this meant parent/child or even sibling to sibling."

Xavier was taken aback but realized there was no other option to save Aria. He took a deep breath and began to try and feel a connection to the father he hated.

"Try repeating sânge la sânge." Kiera told him. "It means blood to blood. Feel him Xavier, feel him, it's okay to use the hate you have for him. Hate is a strong emotion and that is what you need. I think we can give you, our strength." Kiera grasped his hand. Katrina took his other hand, Gabriel put his hands on his shoulders, while Chris, Brian, and Gage closed in around them. Everyone was touching, lending their strength to Xavier.

"You know I'm right; you know your father is a wolf." Tom stepped closer trying to feel if the shield was weakening. But he had underestimated Aria as he had underestimated her mother. She could see the tall blonde colored wolf staring at her and she wondered who the teenage boy was. But while Tom had been talking Aria realized that it did not matter who her biological father was. Joel was there when her mother had given birth to her and Joel had been there for her growing up. Joel was there for her when Tom had killed her mother. Joel was her father in every sense of the word. Tom telling her that Evan was her biological father and wasn't going to erase the last 16 plus years Joel had taken care of her and had been there for her. She decided it was best not to talk, she needed to focus on love, on her shield. She knew it was a mistake to engage Tom.

Chapter 20

Tom studied the girl in the middle of the shield, looking past the regal way she held herself he could see Evan in her. Her hair, the slight twist in her top lip, the girl was definitely Evan's. It infuriated him that Cassie and Tessa had prevented both him and Evan from being with their children. He had taken care of both women. He had also taken care of Cassie's parents. He could hardly believe Natasha was with them the night he killed them. He knew Natasha had something extra just like Tessa had and it made him want her. But after a bad fight in which he had lost his temper and struck her, Natasha had disappeared. It should not have surprised him that Cheri would find a witch wolf if there as one within five hundred miles. Tom had decided to take out Cheri because he feared her. He would have continued on to Katrina and golden boy Gabriel, but he felt the need to return home after he had killed Cheri, her husband, Tessa's parents, and Natasha. Looking back, he wondered if Cheri had survived long enough to spell him. He had crawled down to the car to ensure everyone was dead, but the vehicle was so mangled he had just guessed they were all dead. Aria was strong and he had heard of his son's strength as well. He had to find a way to get this girl. If he took her, he knew his son and Gabriel would follow him to the ends of the earth and back to find her. Then he could separate his son from the Silver Creek Pack. Tom turned at the distant sound of running paw prints, he could tell from the sound it was the Silver Creek pack and not his because he could hear both wolf and bear sounds.

Xavier tried to focus and kept being drawn towards Gage, "I don't understand all I feel is Gage?"

"You're not doing it right," Kiera said. "You should only be attracted to Tom because he has your blood, or well actually you have his blood."

Katrina thought it was strange he was feeling Gage but brushed it off to think about later. "Try focusing not only on your blood tie but Tom himself." Katrina told Xavier.

Xavier focused on the hate that he felt for the part of him that was Tom. The falling snow starting to come down faster was distracting him. Just when he thought he would never be able to make the connection, he felt it. Something snapped into place inside of him and he knew which way to go to find his father, to find Aria. Xavier twisted to the North shifting to his wolf and began to run, everyone followed him. Gabriel stayed neck and neck with Xavier hoping he could protect him from the one enemy he had hoped Xavier would never have to face.

Tom's head whipped around towards the sound of running paws. Aria could hear them too, and her body sang with joy. She had begun to feel fatigue but now help was coming. She watched Tom shift to wolf and sprint towards the west, the other wolves following on his heels. The boy wolf looked back at her once more before following the others. When Xavier and Gabriel burst into the clearing, she let her shield fall and collapsed. Her pack rushed to her. "I'm alright, go. He is getting away." Aria looked at Xavier "I'm sorry Xavier it was Tom, your father." Xavier and Gabriel nuzzled her.

Gabriel shifted, "Katrina, get them to the safety of the cave." He shifted back, and they took off after the fleeing wolves.

Katrina and Kiera stayed behind with Aria. They shifted back to human. They grasp hands and put a shield around themselves.

"This will keep us safe for now." Katrina breathed out her blood pumping through her veins so strong she felt dizzy. "We need a break."

"It takes a lot of energy." Aria reminded her.

"I know. We need to keep it up while we regroup and figure out the best way back to the cave." Snow was swirling around them.

The wind was getting stronger as it whipped up little snow tornados that danced through the clearing.

Katrina and Kiera held onto Aria. "I'm so scared." Aria began to cry, "What if they don't come back?"

"They will," Katrina caressed her head, "they have to." She had to believe it. "We should shift to stay warm." Katrina could feel both Kiera and Aria shivering. "It will also help us if any of the intruders come back." They all jumped when they heard a noise at the edge of the clearing.

Gabriel, Xavier, Brian, Gage, and Chris were gaining on the intruders, when they broke into two groups. Gabriel had them all go after Tom and his companion. He figured the other wolves were fleeing and he had to trust Katrina and the girls would be alright.

They started up the side of a mountain, Gabriel figured that Tom had an escape route. He had to find a way to cut him off. As they continued to climb Gabriel could not stop thinking about Katrina and the girls. He knew he had to focus, just then a shot rang out. Gabriel stopped abruptly, the others almost running into him. They looked around checking each other over. They had just gotten into deeper snow when the shot rang out. Looking around they saw the snow near Gage turning crimson. They pulled him into a nearby cave. Brian and Gabriel shifted to humans. "Shift Gage." Brian ordered. "I can't see how bad it is unless you shift."

"Gage, Brian." Gabriel began, Xavier was nuzzling Gage. Gage and Xavier didn't have the same parents or share a familial blood but when Xavier looked at Gage, he was looking at his brother. Gabriel felt like Gage and Xavier were his sons as well. He was torn but knew if they waited any longer Tom would be out of their reach and they would not be safe.

"I'm alright, it hurts like the fires of hell, but I'm alright." Gage said.

Everyone looked at Brian, "He's right it's not deep. Thankfully he was his bear, and we have thick hides. A bullet has to be better aimed than that. Plus, I don't think it was a large caliber weapon."

"I have to keep going," Gabriel hesitated, "if, you are sure."

"I am." Brian confirmed.

"I'm going with you." Xavier looked at Gabriel with such intensity his blue eyes appeared to be glowing.

Gabriel wanted to say no but his gut told him Xavier should be with him. "All of you stay here with Gage, we will come back for you as soon as we can."

"Be careful," Gage said. They all watched as Gabriel and Xavier slipped out of the cave as humans.

"Mom, Aria look," Kiera exclaimed pointing towards the tree line to their left. Katrina and Aria turned to see the white wolf followed by his pack coming through the trees.

"They are here to protect us." Aria could feel it.

"I agree," Katrina kissed both of their foreheads. "Let's shift."

All three of them shifted, staying huddled together as their shield fell. The white wolf approached them, nudging the sides of their bodies trying to get them all to move.

Katrina stood on four legs, Kiera and Aria followed suit. The wild wolves filed in around them and the white alpha led them all through the storm. Katrina was worried but she sensed the wild wolves were again trying to protect them. Before long Katrina could see the cave with the protection spell. The wild wolves were able to pass through the barrier confirming they had no ill intent.

Aria was in awe of the wild wolves. They were beautiful, alluring, and powerful. She lay next to Katrina when she chose a spot inside the cave. They could clearly see the opening of the cave from where they lay. Kiera lay down on the other side of Katrina. Aria felt safe for the first time since she had heard the glass break in her house, but she was terrified for the other pack members still out there. The wild wolves lay all around them like sentries. When Greg showed up the sentries rose and accessed him. He was shocked to see Katrina, Kiera, and Aria laying in the middle of the wild pack. Two wolves approached Greg, and after looking him over they stepped aside.

Katrina shifted, "They tried to take Aria, but she escaped, when she realized she wouldn't make it here she put up a protection spell." She explained to Greg through shivering teeth, she was not dressed to withstand a snowstorm as a human. "We found her in time, you know those spells take a lot of energy. Gabriel, Xavier, Gage, Chris, and Brian went after the intruders. One of them is Tom."

"I'll go back out and help them as soon as Ryan and Todd get here." Greg said as two more wolves approached. The wild wolves accessed them as they had done to Greg and let them through. Greg and Katrina quickly explained and shifted back as Greg, Ryan, and Todd left to go help their Alpha. The white wolf led the three out and they disappeared in a swirl of snow.

Gabriel and Xavier followed Tom's tracks fearing they had already escaped. They worked their way up and around the side of the mountain as humans. They were just about to turn back when they heard voices. There were three men standing on the edge of a drop off. Gabriel realized it was beginning to snow even harder and the wind was howling. Late spring snowstorms were not uncommon in Silver Creek.

"You idiot. How did they find us?" Tom was berating a woman who was cowering. Gabriel nodded and Xavier snuck around the other side. They were betting Tom would not hurt Xavier. They had decided Xavier would distract Tom and the others. Gabriel would join the fight once Xavier had taken out the man with the gun.

"Why are you here?" Xavier asked, stepping into the clearing. He had to raise his voice over the howling wind.

Tom whirled, recognizing his son instantly. "Xavier."

"Why are you here?" Xavier asked again.

The man started to raise the rifle, "Don't" the command and panic in Tom's voice was strong. The man looked surprised but lowered the rifle. "You belong with me."

"It didn't escape my notice that you went after Aria, not me." Xavier pointed out.

"She is Evan's daughter," Tom explained, "I promised him I would bring his child back to him."

"Your henchman didn't know who she was when they first came for her and Kiera." Xavier countered. "Stop lying."

"Where is your pack, Xavier?" Tom asked. He couldn't believe Gabriel would let his boy follow him alone.

"Someone shot Gage." Xavier said. "I slipped out; Gabriel was too busy tending to Gage to realize I left."

"He will notice soon." Tom warned.

"He will." Xavier agreed, "But I wanted to talk to you." Xavier was in sweatpants and a t-shirt, since he had been in bed when they ran out of the house. His clothing was drenched from the snow, but he didn't notice. Blood and adrenaline were racing through his body, making him unaware of the cold.

"You came to talk? How did you know it was me?" Tom asked.

"I came to talk and kill you, but I'm guessing your henchman there would just shoot me if I tried to attack you." Xavier nodded towards the man with the lowered rifle. "We figured out it was you after you killed Aria's father. She found diaries her mother had written and the men you sent on the last attempt to take Kiera were described in them. Cassie linked you and the men for us."

"Ahhh clever Cassie, still a pain in my ass from the grave." Tom sighed. "You and Aria belong with me and Evan. I will gladly take Gage and the little red she wolf. Gabriel and Katrina will need to go though."

"You sound like you could get rid of them if you tried." Xavier sneered.

"They are useless." Tom spat.

"They raised me." Xavier's words were ice, but on the inside, he was burning.

"THEY STOLE YOU!" Tom yelled.

"YOU KILLED MY MOTHER!" Xavier screamed, letting the fire out. "YOU KILLED MY MOTHER AND I WILL NEVER FORGIVE YOU FOR THAT."

"They killed her." Tom was trying to even his voice. "They killed her because she wanted to be with me."

"Lies." Xavier said. "Stop telling lies."

"Xavier, you and your mother were stolen from me. As Aria was stolen from Evan, her real father." Tom took a step forward. Xavier took an exaggerated step away from Tom that also brought him closer to the man with the rifle. Xavier could tell that Tom thought he could trick him. "Your mother wanted to be with me, but your grandparents kept her away." Tom continued.

"I've been told what happened. My mother wanted to leave you." Xavier began to pace. He was hoping the continued movement would keep them distracted from his real target. "You killed her and would have killed Cassie, but she was too strong for you then. So, you waited and killed her later."

"No," Tom insisted, "Your mother wanted to take you and be with me, but your grandparents wouldn't let her."

Xavier leaped at the man with the rifle changing to wolf in midair. He had to trust Gabriel had his back. When Xavier leapt Gabriel disabled the woman who Tom had been yelling at and went for him. "You have poisoned my son." Tom spat swinging a stick at Gabriel who was now a wolf.

Xavier finally disabled the man with the rifle. He saw Gabriel trying to get an opening on Tom who was swinging the stick. "He is my son not yours." Tom yelled, pulling a handgun from his pocket at the same time Gabriel lunged. A shot rang out as Tom fell over the edge.

Xavier froze accessing the situation. As Gabriel turned, he expected to see blood, instead Gabriel shifted back to human. "He missed."

Xavier ran to him shifting back to human, "Thank God you are alright."

They steadied each other, both injured from the fighting. They walked to the edge but looking over all they saw was swirling white as the storm ratcheted up.

"He's wrong." Gabriel said, looking at Xavier. "You are my son." At a loss for words Xavier gently hugged Gabriel.

"What are we going to do with them?" Xavier asked.

"Leave them."

"Even the woman?" Xavier pointed to where she was laying, "She's gone." He was shocked.

"We aren't going to find her in this mess." Gabriel pointed out. "We'll come see if they are still here after the blizzard. We better get going, we'll be lucky to find our way back in this."

They both shifted to wolf and started back to where they had left Gage, Chris and Brian. They were surprised to find Greg, Todd, Ryan, and the white alpha.

"He led us straight to them." Greg pointed to the white wolf.

"We are grateful." Gabriel told the white wolf.

The white wolf yipped and took a few steps towards the opening of the cave. They all took it as a command to change and follow him. They all went back out into the now raging storm as wolves. The white wolf led them to the protected cave.

Kiera shifted, "What happened?" Kiera shouted as they walked through the entrance of the cave. She ran up to Gage and caressed his side above the wound.

"He's alright." Gabriel said after he shifted. "Shift back Kiera and let's get to the house. I'll explain everything there." Aria and Xavier nuzzled each other. Gabriel nuzzled Katrina as they began to head home escorted by the wild wolf pack, who had become their brethren.

Everyone was exhausted. Aria, Gabriel, and Xavier explained what happened to the pack who had all come after receiving the alert. As each told their story they hoped with Tom out of the picture the rest of the Siberian Pack would leave them alone.

Gabriel, Greg, and the rest of the deputies made sure all of the pack members made it home despite the storm. Gage was resting in one of the bedrooms, Chris watching over him, leaving Gabriel, Katrina, Xavier, Kiera, Aria, and Brian sitting around the fire. The storm was a full-blown blizzard now and it was hard to tell if the sun had risen yet. Everyone had showered and changed into comfy clothes. Katrina had made them hot chocolate. "Do you think Evan will try for me again?" Aria asked. Xavier rubbed her arm as they looked at Gabriel and Katrina.

"We don't know." Gabriel said.

"I think for now we'll be safe." Katrina assured her. "They didn't expect to find us strong. It sounds like Tom thought he could just manipulate everyone. He sure wasn't expecting Aria to be able to produce a shield spell."

"We will go back and check for the men when the storm breaks." Gabriel said.

"How long till the snow melts?" Aria asked Xavier. It had been three days since Aria had raced through the woods failing to reach safety. She was standing on the back deck looking at the snow melting off the trees.

"Within a month you will start to see more solid signs of spring." Xavier answered.

"Do you think they are alive?" Aria asked again. She had asked Xavier this question a hundred times.

"I don't know, there was no sign of them when we went back." Xavier answered without irritation. "Bears have a better smell than even a wolf and we couldn't smell them in either form."

Aria sighed, "I hope they are gone. I never want to meet Evan."

"Hopefully you won't have to." Xavier wrapped his arm around Aria. "Let's focus on something else."

"Agreed." Aria said jumping up from the chair, "Let's go check on Kiera and Gage."

Xavier smiled at her and stood up. Kiera hadn't left Gage's side since they had gotten home. The doctor said Gage would heal but needed to rest so the wound would stop opening back up. They all felt for now the danger was gone. Tom had not likely survived the fall. They felt safe under the theory that when you cut off the head of the monster, the body died too. They held hands as they walked into and through the house. Aria looked back at the large log and river rock home as they walked towards Xavier's truck. This was now Aria's, she would stay here in her ancestral home. She had Xavier, she had Kiera, she had family, and she had a pack.

She knew she had to think about everything she had learned. She would turn seventeen soon, she would be a senior in high school. She wanted to learn more about her heritage and about the family she had grown close to. She knew that more healing had to happen. They would all heal. She smiled as Xavier opened her door. He still made the butterflies dance in her stomach. He gave her a kiss before shutting her door. He walked around the front of the car while Aria admired his long legs clad in jeans and the muscles his black t-shirt showed off.

"You're pretty cute." She told him when he slid into the driver's seat.

"Cute?" He questioned doubtfully. "Future alpha wolves are not cute."

She grinned at him, "well you are" she said with certainty.

"I don't know about you." He poked her in the side as he put the truck in drive.

They were both smiling as they drove towards Gabriel's and Katrina's house to sit with Kiera and Gage. They were together and that was what mattered most.

Epilogue

He had been injured badly and had been in bed for days, when he finally recovered enough to speak, he called for Evan. "I've seen her."

"I know her brother told me." Evan replied.

"He almost gave me away." Tom's voice was dangerous.

"He is a boy seeing his sister for the first time." Evan said unafraid of Tom. "There's something else you should know, I found out while researching them."

"What?" Tom asked the pain starting to become overwhelming,

"The boy Walter shot is yours." Evan said.

Tom went pale, "What, Walter was taken down too, how did he shoot Xavier?"

"No, I was looking through the birth records of the pack. When Natasha left Seattle, she eventually ended up in Missoula where she ran into Cheri." Evan explained.

"I know Cheri took her in, she was in the car the night I ran them off the road." Tom was getting angry, "Are you saying she had a son?"

"She gave birth to a boy about 6 months after she left your apartment in Seattle. She lived in a shelter a little east of Seattle for about a year, then moved east to Spokane. She lived there for about another year then made her way into Missoula where she met Cheri." Evan laid it out. "She was pregnant when she ran just like Cassie. When the Silver Creek pack took her in, they also took in her two-year-old son."

"Did he live?" Tom demanded turning red.

"Yes, he did," Evan reassured him. "I'll leave you now, you look tired and have a lot of healing to do."

Tom lay there thinking, he had two sons, two strong healthy young men. He knew it would take months for him to heal his broken body. He was broken from going over the cliff, but when he healed, he would find his sons. He decided he would find them and convince them to join him. He fell asleep picturing the day his sons joined him.

Silver Skies Coming in 2025

Natasha tiptoed out of the house. Even though he wasn't there she was afraid of being too loud. She had a backpack and some money she had been secretly taking from him when she dared and nothing else. It would be a hike to the bus station but so long as he didn't leave work early, she would be well out of Seattle before he arrived home and realized that she had gone. She was a block away from the apartment before her heart rate started to slow. She made it to the bus station and got situated. As the bus left Seattle, she felt her body relax further. She rested her hand on her stomach. He didn't know about the life growing inside of her. He would never know about the life growing inside of her, she promised herself silently. She'd thought he was so handsome and charming but as soon as she moved in with him, he'd changed. He became abusive and violent. She had been planning to leave for months, she would not live as someone's punching bag. Once she realized she was pregnant two months after she moved in, she knew she had to get out as fast as she could. The child was hers alone now and he would never know. She rested her head against the window using her sweatshirt as a pillow. As the bus started down Snoqualmie pass, she drifted into a fitful sleep filled with memories.

She was a dark streak running over pure white snow. She finally stopped and looked around. She'd lost the wolves chasing her. She was small and fast but still thought it was incredible luck that the ice behind her had begun to crack. She had gone at least five miles past the river where she guessed she'd lost her pursuers. She hoped they'd gone through the ice and been trapped beneath it. She hadn't turned back to look since it would've slowed her down. She thought about running to the nearest village but decided that was the first place they'd look for her. She turned south and began to trot at a steady pace. She made it 20 miles before curling up in a snowbank to sleep. As she turned in circles to find a comfortable spot, gentle snowflakes began to fall.

It took her 3 days traveling 15-25 miles a day to make it to the city of Chernivtsi in the Ukraine. She'd been lucky enough to catch a few mice and rabbits so she wasn't as hungry as she'd thought she would be. She shifted to her human form; it took her a bit to acclimate back to human. She'd never spent so many days as a wolf without shifting at all before. She found a place to sleep at a local hostel. Once she got settled, she began to plan. She would get to the states and start a new life if it's the last thing she did.

About the Authors

Jackie Bennett is originally from a small town in Northern Wisconsin. She moved to the Twin Ports when she was young. In her former life Jackie was an over the road truck driver with her husband. She spent hours traveling all over the United States and Canada listening to audiobooks and chatting about them with Clover. She retired from the open road when she had her first daughter. She now has three children, and she loves sharing her passion for books with her kids. Although audiobooks are still her go to source for a great story, she does love the feel of holding a book in her hands. Along with her family, including their adorable dog Doug, she loves to explore state and national parks and enjoy the great outdoors. Her family holds a special place in her heart, and she gets her inspiration from them.

Clover Bennett was a bit of a wild child growing up. She loved to climb trees, jump off lighthouses into Lake Superior, and had no problem telling people what she thought. It's only fitting that at the age of 19 she left her hometown and ran off with a U. S. Marine to see the world and create her own exciting adventures. Her journey took her far and wide and eventually brought her back home where she and Jackie now share their dream of being a dynamic writing duo creating exciting adventures for others to read. Now she enjoys a quiet life in the middle of the Wisconsin woods with her amazing husband, dogs, cats, and occasionally a flock of chickens.